THE DUKE'S SPINSTER
Duke Dare, Book 1

Eliana Piers

© Copyright 2025 by Eliana Piers
Text by Eliana Piers
Cover by Dar Albert

Dragonblade Publishing, Inc. is an imprint of Kathryn Le Veque Novels, Inc.
P.O. Box 23
Moreno Valley, CA 92556
ceo@dragonbladepublishing.com

Produced in the United States of America

First Edition January 2025
Trade Paperback Edition

Reproduction of any kind except where it pertains to short quotes in relation to advertising or promotion is strictly prohibited.

All Rights Reserved.

The characters and events portrayed in this book are fictitious. Any similarity to real persons, living or dead, is purely coincidental and not intended by the author.

ARE YOU SIGNED UP FOR DRAGONBLADE'S BLOG?

You'll get the latest news and information on exclusive giveaways, exclusive excerpts, coming releases, sales, free books, cover reveals and more.

Check out our complete list of authors, too!

No spam, no junk. That's a promise!

Sign Up Here

www.dragonbladepublishing.com

Dearest Reader;

Thank you for your support of a small press. At Dragonblade Publishing, we strive to bring you the highest quality Historical Romance from some of the best authors in the business. Without your support, there is no 'us', so we sincerely hope you adore these stories and find some new favorite authors along the way.

Happy Reading!

CEO, Dragonblade Publishing

CHAPTER ONE

THIS IS WHAT it must feel like to be drunk. If not drunk, exactly, then definitely a little...tingly. Lady Boudicca had never been drunk before, but surely, this fuzzy feeling must be part of it. There must have been something in the tepid lemonade because, of all the four sisters in the Rochester clan, Boudicca would never have taken a drink of her own volition.

Artemisia, her youngest sister? Yes. The third youngest, Joan? Probably. Zenobia, second in line? Probably not. Boudicca? Definitely not. And they all knew it.

It was one of the reasons why she could almost be their chaperone. That, and she was six-and-twenty years of age now. A veritable spinster. Men hadn't cast glances at her since, well, since she'd been shelved at the ripe old age of three-and-twenty. And they still weren't looking tonight.

"Nobi, stop ogling Christopher," Joan nudged her sister. "You do realize that you're not discreet about it."

Zenobia blushed.

"She can't help it. She's in love," Artemisia drawled the last word as only the baby of the family could do.

Boudicca took another sip of the bland lemonade.

"You do realize that the lemonade is spiked, Bodi." Artemisia held up her glass and gulped it down.

Blame the drink or her bad mood, but Boudicca did not hold herself responsible for her petulant response, "Don't call me that ridiculous name. There are no ladies with such a vulgar name."

"There are no ladies with our names at all. Blame our parents for that one."

"It was mostly Father. What with his love for battle strategy. Do you really believe Mother would have chosen these warrior names for her dainty daughters?" *Dainty* would have sounded sarcastic if it hadn't dripped from Joan's lips.

"Just let her be, Mimi. Bodi—I mean Boudicca—is obviously in a poor temperament." Zenobia patted Boudicca's forearm and gave each of the bookended sisters a knowing glance.

"You're right." Artemisia smiled. "But just because you're happily in love, doesn't mean the rest of us are."

The red in Zenobia's cheeks returned. "I wouldn't quite say *happy*. Or *love*."

Artemisia blew a raspberry with her lips.

"Mimi," Boudicca hissed.

"Please. She's halfway down the aisle." If they hadn't been in a ballroom, Boudicca would have expected Artemisia to stick out her tongue. Never mind, they were in a ballroom, and Mimi still managed to stick out her tongue.

Zenobia shook her head. "There won't be any aisle."

"Well, not if you don't make a move. He's too slow to see—"

"He's not slow."

"All right, he's too...much of a man"—Artemisia eyed Zenobia for approval on her verbal amendment—"to notice you pining after him. You're going to have to be the one who makes the first move."

Zenobia scoffed. "That's never going to happen."

"You can't be timid. This is your life, Zenobia, you have to do something."

Boudicca had heard it all before. It was no secret that Zenobia was in love with their brother's best friend, Christopher, the Duke of Saxby. But, as with all the times before, she was too much of a lady to do anything about it.

"She's right, Nobi." Joan was huddling the sisters. "This is your life. Don't you want to be married to him?"

Zenobia chewed on her bottom lip. "I do." She took a sip of lemonade, which, Boudicca realized now she should be denying her sisters. "But I don't see how that's going to happen."

"It's easy." Artemisia stood, battle ready. She could have had one hand waving a tribe flag in the air, or raising a spear, or blowing a trumpet. Thankfully no said props were readily at hand. "I dare you to tell him how you feel."

Zenobia gasped. "I couldn't."

"What are we, twelve?" Boudicca had to step in. This was moving past ridiculous into scandalous.

"I said what I said." Artemisia crossed her arms and glared at Zenobia. "And we've never balked at a dare."

"They've never been this...this..."

"Important?" Artemisia supplied.

"Scandalous," Boudicca countered.

"Risk not, gain not." May as well have been embroidered on Mimi's flag.

"Who are you, Mimi? Or maybe I should be asking, what's gotten into you tonight?" Boudicca held up the lemonade.

"Call it spirits, but I call it the truth." She turned to Zenobia. "You know you need to do something."

And then, right before her eyes, Boudicca watched a veil lift from Nobi's eyes.

"I'll do it," Zenobia's face hardened. "But—" she lifted her finger and pointed at the other three. "I'll not do it alone. I dare each of you to claim your own duke as well." Where were flags when one needed them?

"What?" Boudicca's heart banged against her chest. Once. Hard. She thought it was done. It was not. The banging banged again in a rhythm she had never heard banged out before.

Artemisia laughed. "I'm in. If that's what it'll take for you to claim the love of your life, then I'm in." Boudicca thought she saw something flash across Mimi's face, but she couldn't decipher it.

Zenobia pointed at Joan, "You've been quiet. Are you in? If I tell Christopher how I feel, will you follow through on my dare?"

Joan shrugged her shoulders, but her shoulders didn't even have time to drop before Artemisia clamored in, saying, "She's in too." She peered at Boudicca. "And Bodi's in too."

"I'm not."

"Yes, you are. You out of all us need a duke the most. In fact, you're going first."

"I don't need a duke."

"Everyone needs a duke," Artemisia laughed.

"I'm a spinster. You three go ahead with this silly dare. I'm the chaperone." Boudicca was about to cross her arms and then remembered where they were.

"Oh no. You're not sitting out on this one. This is your life too. You deserve to be happy." Artemisia wasn't backing down.

"Marrying a duke does not guarantee happiness."

"Not marrying a duke doesn't guarantee happiness either."

Trust the youngest to apply that kind of logic.

"Bodi, I think you should do it." Joan intervened. "You've got nothing to lose."

That stung.

She knew Joan wasn't being intentionally mean. Joan, of all her sisters, was kindness personified. But still, hearing those words pierced through a layer of her heart she thought she had closed off.

She was a spinster. She had accepted it. But to hear the words that she had nothing to lose sounded as if she had already lost.

Well, she hadn't lost. *Yet.* Besides, if she was going first, and she failed, then maybe none of them would go ahead with the silly dares.

Not following through on the dares *would* make chaperoning easier.

ANOTHER NIGHT. ANOTHER crush. Another failure.

Wesley, the Duke of Baskim, had just finished dancing with a diamond of the first water. And he had already forgotten her name. To be honest, he wasn't paying attention to much of the ballroom either. It looked like every other one he'd been to. Candle lights in sconces. Fresh flowers—roses, he could see that much—in enormous bouquets. Footmen hurrying trays about. It was just another ball. And it was nice. But nothing to notice.

"What was wrong with that one?" Samuel eyed the blonde he had just danced with. At least, he thought it was the same woman.

"She had nothing to say."

"And that's a problem because...?"

"You may not need conversation in your future, but I'd like to have some kind of stimulation. I think Chris and James would back me up on that one. No?"

"I want conversation. Actually, I even think it'd be ideal to marry my best friend." Chris murmured the last phrase, "If that were possible."

"Conversation sounds great. Not as great as some other things though." James grinned.

"Thank you, Chris." Wesley tilted his head at one of his friends.

"All I'm saying is that you find something wrong with every woman you meet. You just need to pick one, and get an heir. Society may think you're Adonis incarnate, but you're the oldest of all of us." Samuel rocked back and forth on his heels.

"I'm not even halfway through my thirties. I have time."

"Hardly."

But truth be told, Wesley was starting to feel slight tremors of desperation. Of all the ladies he had met, not a single one had captured his attention for more than a dance. Perhaps it was time to just make a choice. He had had enough of women flocking to his good locks and deep pockets.

"If you know the ladies so well, why don't you just choose

one for me?" It was an impulsive thing to say, but Wesley said it anyway.

Samuel rubbed his hands together. "Now, there's the best idea you've had all night. Indeed, quite possibly the best idea you've ever had. You're too damn picky. If my recollection serves, you haven't given a single lady a second chance. The three of us can most certainly do a better job on your love life than you."

"Not my love life, just my married life." Wesley was irritated. Samuel *would* make this a competition. Everything was a competition with him. Often Wesley won. Then again, often Samuel won. So really, it was an ongoing, never-ending battle between them.

Wesley watched as Samuel's eyes scanned the ballroom. And he watched as they landed on another diamond in the water a few feet away from him. A brunette. This time, although he didn't remember the name, he remembered that she was secretly promised to another duke. He hadn't inquired so much as she had told him. With the obvious intent to (unnecessarily) ward off any further advances from him. Amused at the memory, Wesley felt his spirits lift.

Knowing any initiatives with her wouldn't last, he felt pity (or was it glee), and figured he may as well give his opponent a shot.

"You have to propose to the next lady you bump into."

"I'm not going to propose to some random lady of your choosing tonight."

Samuel hadn't taken his eyes off of the brunette. "Not tonight. Tonight you dance. Then you finally give a woman a second chance: you court. Then you propose. If she refuses you...then..."

"Then what?"

"I guess you win this one."

"Those stakes are awfully high. And one-sided. What do I get if I win?"

Samuel lowered his voice and stated his stakes.

Chris and James, who had otherwise only been listening, gasped. "What? Why would you do that?"

"I like a good bet. And I like to win," Samuel shrugged.

The bet was preposterous. There was no good reason Samuel would bet *that*. Was there?

It also seemed too easy. Wesley weighed the risks in his mind. He knew the brunette would say no. He knew he would win. Really, he had nothing to lose.

So, with the odds obviously in his favor, Wesley shook Samuel's hand.

CHAPTER TWO

Now all he had to do was bump into Lady Simone, ask her to dance, and have a sham courtship.

The details of the bet had been set. Bump into a lady. Dance with her. Court her. Propose to her. And of course, she wasn't allowed to know of the bet. That would throw everything off. To Samuel, it wasn't part of the bet if the woman said yes or no to the proposal. Likely, he assumed the woman would say yes, because really, what woman would say no to him?

He was a handsome, wealthy, young duke. And he had a decent personality. Or, more precisely, up until this time, his personality hadn't been harsh enough to deter any ladies.

Speaking of not deterring ladies, there was Her Grace, the dowager Duchess of Melson. She was making a beeline for him. He knew what that entailed. She had already tried to set him up with several ladies. How many nieces, god-daughters, and other female relatives of marrying age could one woman have?

Apparently, the answer was infinite. For they just kept coming. And each one that came gave him a new headache.

The first one had spelled her name for him. Her name had been Jane. *Jane with an e*, she had said. The dance couldn't have been short enough after that opener. The next one wasn't sure where the continent was. The entire continent. She wasn't sure if England was north of it, south, east, or west.

The next few ladies the dowager had finagled a dance for

were ruthless gossips. He still wasn't sure what their angle was. Should he be impressed that they knew so much about the *ton* that they could recite whose dresses were a season out of style? Or was he supposed to commiserate with them and lament the deterioration of society as one knew it all because one wore too much lace? Or was it ribbons?

And after that, Wesley hadn't kept a very clear record of who was who. All he knew was that he dreaded the sight of the dowager, and he avoided her at all costs.

So, with her in sight, and he with a game plan for at least part of the evening, he strategized a getaway. In theory, it should be simple. Keep an eye on her while backing up just enough to make a quick turn and dart toward Lady Simone. Then commence the bumping.

If only theories always worked the way they should...well, then science as the world knew it would be an entirely different game. The theory worked as far as keeping his eyes on her and backing up.

"Wesley, are you—" Samuel had a smirk on his face as he darted a glance between Wesley and the duchess.

He was smirking because he knew what was coming if Wesley didn't make a clean escape. And, of course, instead of aiding and abetting the runner, Samuel lifted two fingers to acknowledge—and welcome!—the dowager.

"Traitor," Wesley hissed and flashed angry blue eyes at his friend. In response, Samuel's wavy long locks jostled in laughter. Wielding a bit of a rebellious streak, Samuel was the only one in their posse with longer hair. The other three could almost pass for brothers, with Wesley being the most uptight of them. And right now, Wesley was especially resentful of the mischief in his friend's countenance. That man could play dirty when he wanted to. And there was a lot at stake.

Flustered, Wesley took a few extra steps backward, therefore making his swift turn further away from his intended target, and—

THUNK!

Drat. Something soft and pliable met his elbow. And then something lukewarm and wet dripped down the back of his calf.

This was the last thing he needed. Some over imbibing imbecile throwing his drink all over his breeches.

Mid-turn, heart hammering, all to avoid the dowager and engage in this already irritating bet, Wesley started to confront the man who was obviously at fault. "What the deuc—" and mid-thought he realized the voice leaking an expletive didn't belong to a man at all, but a lady. "—duke?"

And if Wesley hadn't been flustered beyond belief, trying to avoid the dowager at all costs, as well as working his way to Lady Simone who liked him less than he liked her (which should have been an affront to his ego but was not), he probably would have noticed a few things about the lady holding the lemonade.

"I beg your pardon, Your Grace," the sweet voice drifted over his head.

"Never mind. Just—just...needs to be cleaned up." He wasn't looking at her downcast head of golden locks as he scanned the room for a footman.

Catching the eye of one, he raised his handkerchief saying, "Here."

The lady then looked up and saw the raised cloth. A flash of umbrage flew across her eyes. She snatched the cloth with a grumble he couldn't make out.

Shocked that she snatched his handkerchief from his fingers, he snapped at her, "What are you doing?"

"Am I too slow, Your Grace?" she bit off. All sweetness evaporated.

"No, of course not."

She bent down before he could say another word and placed the cloth on the ground to soak up the liquid.

"Get up," he grumbled.

"Would you make up your mind?" she volleyed.

Nettled, he took her hand in his. A current shot through him, but he was far too vexed to give it much credence. "Stop that," he ground out. "You'll make a scene."

"Anything but a scene, Your Grace." She curtsied, but he couldn't help but feel it was a mocking tone.

What did he care? Finish the curtsy and be gone. He had a bet to work on.

The woman stood and glared at him with the clearest blue eyes he had ever seen. And then she was gone.

Thank God. He sighed and started to head toward Lady Simone.

"Ahem," Samuel cleared his throat, suddenly appearing beside him. "Aren't you going to ask her to dance?" He smiled coyly. "Oh, I see, you're playing a game first. All the power to you."

"What game? What dance?" Wesley furrowed his brows.

Samuel merely flicked his wrist toward the woman with the lemonade splattered hem.

"What about her?" Wesley didn't have time for this. He needed to go bump into Lady Simone.

"She's the one you bumped into first, isn't she?"

Panic shot through Wesley. Pure, undiluted panic. It rippled up from his toes and settled between his shoulders.

"That. Was. Not. A. Bump."

"You backed up into her elbow did you not? Physical contact was made and all that." Samuel was grinning like a lunatic. Like a triumphant lunatic.

"I'm telling you, it wasn't a bump."

"No? What would you call it?" Samuel turned to Chris and James, both mirroring each other's expression. That is, tight lips and raised brows. "Chris? James? Was it a bump?"

"I'm staying out of this one," Chris said.

James merely shrugged. "Could have been."

"It wasn't a bump," Wesley maintained for the third time. As if saying something three times made it true. "It was a thunk."

Samuel belted a laugh. "That's classic." He slapped Wesley on the shoulder. "Twisting the bet to your favor at your whim." He shook his head. "I should have known that you would renege."

"I'm not reneging on anything," he spoke through gritted teeth. "If you want to call that a bump," he forced the words out, "then call it a bump."

"I did." Samuel shot the three a wide grin. "I declare that was a bump. *The* bump. Let's be clear." His eyes narrowed. "That's the lady."

That *thunk* apparently had been *the bump* that sealed Wesley's fate.

WHAT THE DUKE? The pompous invective echoed in Boudicca's ears like a gong being repeatedly hit over and over again, not even giving time for the reverberations to complete their rounds. What kind of arrogant arse was vain enough to curse using his own title? Of all the haughty, self-important, egotistical things she had ever heard, that had to sit at the top. In fact, it sat high above the rest. For a man to equate himself to a deity…it rankled, and it rankled deep. Deeper than the shivering that had shot through her when he grabbed her hand. Deeper than where that shot had settled between her thighs.

Ugh. That man. That duke. Her sisters could choose any duke except that one, and she would play along. Of course she would be steering him ultimately to a rejection, but she would play along with her sisters' dare just long enough to satisfy them.

"Bodi," Mimi squealed in her ear. "The Duke of Baskim. Aiming high. I love it."

"I'm not aiming for the Duke of Baskim."

"Who are you going to snag then?" Nobi queried.

"No one," she answered before she thought it through.

"But you said you would do the dare first. You can't back out now. It's not even been five minutes." Mimi's eyes were hard and her jaw was set. "You're supposed to be our example."

It hadn't even been five minutes? Ha. It felt as though it had been five hours. There was no duke on her mind for herself.

"Come on Bodi," Joan's quiet voice stirred something in her. "You don't have to make the first move."

Boudicca scoffed. "If I don't make the first move, trust me, nothing is going to happen. I've been on the shelf for a few years now. I'd have to tackle a duke to be seen at this point."

Her sisters chuckled. "No tackling will be necessary. I'm sure if you drop your fan at just the right moment, a gentlemanly duke will pick it up for you."

"Or tip your foil at him, trapping him in a corner. That would surely get you enough gossip to start your fencing school for girls," Zenobia whirled her finger in the air like a small blade.

"I'm not ready for that yet." Boudicca tightened her smile, not wanting to let on how much she wished she was there. Ready to open her school for girls.

Thankfully, to distract her, the ridiculous flirtation brought to mind the duke and his handkerchief on the ground. She still couldn't believe he had asked her to clean it up. He had crashed into her after all. She was lucky she was still on her feet. What had he been doing walking backward like that anyway? She shook her head at the vexatious man.

"What about the Duke of Baskim?" Joan asked innocently. "You two were talking. What happened?"

"Nothing happened." And nothing ever would.

"Did he ask you to dance?" Nobi piped up.

"No, of course not."

"There's no *of course not* about it. He could have asked you to dance." Mimi was practically hopping back and forth on her feet in front of Boudicca in excitement.

"Well, he didn't."

"He could have," Mimi returned.

"Not in any known universe—"

"Well, what if he did? What would you say?"

Three sets of eyes were on Boudicca awaiting her answer. She couldn't very well say that she would sabotage the dare. She had to give them hope.

"If"—she held up her index finger—"If he *ever* asked me to dance...I would say yes."

The three sisters squealed. A whisper squeal.

Of course he would never ask, so there was no concern that she was giving them false hope.

CHAPTER THREE

WESLEY LIKED FOOD. Perhaps slightly more than the average person. Perhaps not more than the average man though. He didn't have any peculiar preferences. Sure, he liked beef over chicken. A rare cooked beef over one well done. And just the right lobster could top that. He always ate the food in front of him and always ate dessert. Ever since he was a small child, he had been that way. Various textures didn't faze him. Though he knew some people who couldn't stand the silky-smooth texture of tripe, it didn't bother him. Anything, if cooked well, could taste quite delicious.

But if there was one thing he despised swallowing, it was his own pride.

So it was taking him a little longer than he would have liked to choke it down. Leaning against the wall, taking a sip from his champagne, he knew his next move. Walk over to the bumpable spinster. Bumpable. That was surely not a word. What did it even mean in this scenario? He *had* been the one to bump into her, so perhaps she was bumpable. Or had she bumped into him? Had Samuel known it? Expected it? Planned it, even? He wouldn't put it past him, though he wasn't sure how Samuel could have orchestrated it all so smoothly.

Wesley grumbled. It was probably all a ploy, but now that he was in it, he wanted to win. In all his years, he would have never expected Samuel to wager what he had.

Now all Wesley had to do was propose. Of course, he would only propose trusting she would say no.

He reviewed his plan. Walk over to her. Ask her to dance. It was so simple. She couldn't say no. Not only because he was a duke (because really, what kind of woman would say no to a duke?) but also because it violated the highest regarded value of the *ton*: etiquette. If a man asked a woman to dance, she had to accept unless she was otherwise engaged in a dance or if she was injured. He had wondered a time or two at the veracity of an opportune megrim or turned ankle. But the clear-eyed, bumpable spinster (one had to think she was a spinster by her maturity) appeared to be in good health. From his short encounter with her.

Inwardly he groaned so loud he had to grip his glass a little bit tighter to keep everything inside. Though not prone to irrational actions as such, he was not impervious to them either.

As he observed the woman, he saw her surrounded by three other women. All of whom appeared to be younger than her. They were likely her sisters. Two blondes, two brunettes. From his distance it was hard to tell much more than that, but even from yards away he could see a family resemblance in their facial structure and figures.

All he could think was that hopefully this spinster was not prone to fits. If there was one thing he couldn't stand, it was a woman given to hysterics. And as long as she wasn't mousy, he could have a conversation with her and it wouldn't be unbearable to make good on this bet.

Oh, and another thing, she had better not be a bluestocking. All he needed was for a woman to talk his ears off, spouting some unfounded political ideals. She also better not bore him to death about fashion. Hang it all, the list could go on…he had better just meet the cursed gel and get it over with.

He pushed himself off the wall, took a deep breath, and—not quite able to conjure a smile—he at least forced a scowl off his lips.

"Good evening," he said evenly to the four-woman coterie.

The spinster narrowed her eyes at him while the other three chorused, "Your Grace," followed by curtsies.

"It's a fine evening for a ball. I do hope you're enjoying the event." It was blase, but it was the most effort his head was willing to put forth.

"We are," the other blonde, who appeared to be the youngest, spoke first. Nudging her spinster sister, she continued. "It's a lovely evening for *dancing*."

Subtle.

Well, he certainly couldn't say he hadn't seen the same before. Or worse. He shuddered at a memory. Much worse.

"I fear I'm at a disadvantage, for I have yet to be introduced to all four of you." He had better work up a little more charm. "Missing one might be understandable, but having not been introduced to any of you indicates gross negligence." That earned him a couple of smiles from the brunettes along with a soft chuckle from the youngest blonde.

"I'm Lady Artemisia. These are my sisters, Lady Boudicca," she pointed to the spinster, "Lady Joan and Lady Zenobia."

He would have applauded any man for maintaining his stoicism at the mention of four fierce female warriors. As for himself, he couldn't keep one of his eyebrows in place.

Boudicca, now that he knew her name, was peering past him. Apparently uninterested in the conversation. Not many women had the audacity to show such disregard. She was treating him as if she were his superior. As though to get back at him for something. Though he knew not what that was. Regardless, he had a goal he needed to complete.

"May I have the next dance, Lady Boudicca?" He extended his hand to her, hearing the final strains of the music. For a fleeting moment, there was an alarm bell ringing in his head at the suspicion she might decline. It took altogether too long for her to meet his hand. And, if he was correct in his observations, she only did so under the stare and a cough or two from her sisters.

Odd, that.

"Of course," she lifted those clear blue eyes to his, "I should be delighted. Above all else."

Her phrasing was off-putting. It was as though she were being sarcastic. She *should* be delighted, but was she?

He was about to find out.

With a firm clasp on her gloved fingers, he led her to the floor. There was an energy about her that wasn't quite restless, but it was fervid. It was an intensity he had not matched up against, except maybe with Samuel. Yet he had no idea what her intensity was aimed at. Him, he supposed. Positive or negative, it was yet to be seen.

"Your sisters are charming." What better way to engage conversation than complimenting a person's family.

"Yes." The word hung in the air like a cloud of smoke one wasn't expecting in a crowded ballroom. There were spaces for clouds of smoke, and this wasn't it. "They are." Another puff of smoke.

He almost choked on the awkwardness, but he had experienced worse. Her shortage of words appeared deliberate, which meant he needed to find out why. Or if he was unable to determine her motivation, he would at least need to break her out of it.

"They must have learned their charm from you," he smirked.

"Why would you say that?" It was the scowl that gave her away. Well, that and the tone. She was offended. Again.

"You're the eldest, aren't you?"

Her response was a harrumph.

"Surely, you taught them all they know."

"I may have, or I may not have."

"May I inquire as to the origin of your effrontery? Is it me? Or is this your default demeanor?"

The odds were essentially in thirds. She could have answered affirmatively, negatively, or remained mum on the subject. So he should have had some expectation that she would be direct, yet he had no such preconceived notions.

So when she avowed, "I can assure you that it is you," he merely threw back his head and laughed.

"And what exactly have I done to offend you? Perhaps I should apologize for bumping into you?"

"You didn't bump into me. You crashed into me."

He had never in all his life been so thrown off in the middle of a dance as to stop mid-step, but at those words he ceased hearing the three-four timing of the waltz. The strings were silenced. And his ears no longer perceived the resounding keys.

"That's exactly what I told them," he stared at her, feeling all kinds of odd. Had he not just tried to convince his friends that the bump they were calling a bump was in fact not a bump at all? And here Boudicca was vindicating him.

"Your Grace," she murmured. And the pressure from her fingers, the darting of her eyes, and the brush of her skirts against his thigh all thrummed through him reminding him that he was in the middle of a dance floor and he had better damn well dance. But it was more than a reminder. It was…something. He couldn't put his finger on it. He wasn't even sure he knew entirely what to put his finger on.

"What did you say? And to whom?" It was the first genuine question she had asked him. He could finally hear the real tone of her voice. It was…crisp. What an odd word to use to describe a voice, but it was. She was crisp.

And then he remembered to answer her question. "I said nothing." He couldn't very well tell her what he had said about the bumping. That would lead to more questions, and he held a very strong conviction (even upon his brief experiences with her) that she would interrogate him. She wouldn't stop until she had discovered the bet. And that would mean he would lose. That would not do. So a small lie was justifiable.

He was pretty sure he heard her mumble, "And so shall I." And they were back to square one. Her shackling him in silence. But that one glimpse into her true self…that one authentic inquiry had given him an outline of who she might actually be. And she might actually be a little bit of fun to draw out. And though his goal was to win, it couldn't hurt to have a little fun in doing so.

So to flaunt his chains, and taunt her, he said, "Your silence shackles me, for it's impossible to have a conversation with myself while maintaining my reputation for sanity. Is this your version of, 'Let the men live in slavery if they will?'" He quoted her namesake trusting she would recognize it, and she didn't disappoint him.

She quirked a brow at him, but gave little else. "I'm merely an 'ordinary person', Your Grace."

"Somehow I doubt that." He lifted his hand, guiding her into a twirl. And as he did so, he caught a glimmer of a smile. A half smile to be sure, but the flash appeared to be genuine all the same.

The dance was coming to an end, and he wouldn't offer for a second one. Not tonight. But he still wanted to plant the seed of his intentions in her mind.

"I shall call on you tomorrow."

"As you wish, Your Grace."

Her deferential treatment should have pleased him. If that was all she had presented to him, it probably would have gratified him. However, knowing what fierceness lay beneath induced a twisted need to see more.

No, she was certainly not ordinary. That fact was spelled out in her very name. If only he knew then that she was one of the least ordinary people he would ever meet, perhaps he could have prepared for his future. As it was, he was the least prepared he could possibly be.

Chapter Four

Men always had ulterior motives. If they told you they wanted one thing, they always wanted another thing. To be sure, they probably wanted that one thing as well, but there was always something else.

So when the Duke of Baskim invited Boudicca to dance, she knew he wanted more than just a dance. There was no reasonable explanation for his arrogant-clean-the-floor-behavior to evolve into a polite-shall-we-dance-because-you're-oh-so-charming demeanor. Definitely not. The man wanted something. What the deuce that was, she didn't know. Yet. But he could be sure that she wouldn't stop until she uncovered the ugly truth. For it was always ugly.

Truth rarely, if ever, came in a neat little box with pretty ribbons. It was never absolutely beautiful. Truth was wrapped in complexities like pain, vulnerabilities, and weakness. All the things Boudicca cared little for.

After years on the Marriage Mart, she had experienced her fair share of *truthful* men, only later to discover their ulterior motives. Fortune hunters. Pleasure seekers. Status climbers. Lord Tamely—not as tame as his name would suggest—was the worst of the lot. He had a habit of making full families his enemy. Thankfully, she had escaped his clutches. Unfortunately, it had to happen more than once. He wasn't the only culprit though. She was an earl's daughter with a more than fair dowry. And she could admit with confidence that she was beautiful. So despite her family's eccentric reputation, there had been offers. Not a single one of which she had considered for even a second. It hadn't been difficult to convince her father of that either.

He was around. But not very attentive. Or attentive at all. Since losing his wife years earlier, he had retreated into his reading. Which mostly consisted of history, strategies for war, and notable quotes from famous warriors, including each daughter's namesake. Much of the knowledge had been passed down (that was putting it lightly, it had been required study) to his daughters and his one son. Boudicca's brother was less present and therefore less attentive than her father, being on the continent and all. The loss of their mother had hit him hard. Perhaps being the only son, he didn't feel as though he could confide in his younger sisters. Though he was treated similarly to his sisters, he was the heir, so it had been different. He had studied as well, but he had also been trained to be the next earl.

Boudicca didn't much mind the obscure studying, the reading, and the memorizing their father forced upon them. But her real passion was in the weaponry. In fact, all the daughters had developed an enthusiasm for one weapon or another.

It was not common knowledge among the *ton*. Heaven forbid gossip got out that the four daughters of an earl spent their off evenings wielding foils, bows, daggers, and pistols. Boudicca's favorite weapon was the long blade. She had been fencing for as long as she could remember, and she was exceptional. Though no one knew it was her behind the mask. It was all part of her grand plan for her life as a spinster. If she was going to be a spinster, she might as well be an eccentric one.

Whenever she worked up an appetite for competition, which was more often than she liked to admit as a woman, she messaged her old fencing tutor to come for a visit. So really, she still had regular lessons almost once a week.

And she was in the middle of writing just such a missive when the butler announced that there was a visitor for her.

A visitor. She knew who it was, of course. The dark-chocolate-haired, hazelnut-eyed duke. The vision of him caused an odd sensation to trickle through her. Hunger. Thinking of food like that was always quick to tempt her appetite.

It would be normal, expected even, for her to take her time. Check her hair. Possibly even change her frock. But him...that arrogant duke, she did nothing. She didn't even check her reflection in the mirror.

She marched downstairs, ready to greet him in the drawing room. No chaperone required. She was spinster enough to be the chaperone.

In her mind, she planned to claim allergies to the flowers he presented, and then offer him lukewarm tea. Even if he brought her favorite bouquet: pale pink peonies. It was as devious as she risked to be. There was no point in making an enemy of the man. She merely wanted to make a good enough show to her sisters that she had hooked a duke. Then, after reeling him in a bit, she would throw him back in the pond for someone else.

The bothersome man couldn't even let her have that.

Upon entering the space, he stood in the middle of the room as if he owned it, hands clasped behind his back. Waiting. Ready. One might even say battle-ready. He was as rigid as the stones used to build her house, and there were no cracks showing.

"Good morning, Lady Boudicca." He smiled and gestured for her to sit. In her own drawing room.

Of all the—

"I hope you're feeling well today. I should love to discuss—"

But there would be no discussion. Her nose sniffed the air. Nothing. Oh, not nothing. A hint of sandalwood. But there was a distinct lack of anything floral, so she tuned him out completely. As her eyes skimmed across the room, she noticed a glaring lack of flowers. The man was a duke. A duke?! He knew to send flowers to a lady he had danced with the previous night. It was etiquette. Pure and simple. If he was not even willing to display the simplest of humilities—argh!—the man had far too much pride. Well, this would just not do.

She raised a hand, palm up, "Did you not bring me flowers?" Clear cut. Direct. There was no other way. The man needed to be taken down a peg or four.

"Flowers?" It was one word, but the tone implied that she couldn't possibly be serious.

"Yes."

She let the silence hang in the air. It was one of the best negotiating tactics she had gleaned over the years.

"You wanted flowers?"

"Did I want flowers?" Echoing the last few words of her opponent's sentence. Another tactic.

"Yes." And as if that single word jostled him out of some nebulous cloud of pretension, he clumsily added, "Of course, I should have brought flowers. How...ungentlemanly of me to forget."

"You forgot?" She wasn't calling him out on a lie...exactly.

He scowled, and she watched his jaw clamp shut. Miraculously, he still managed to grind out a few words. "I apologize."

Not a few. Two. He managed two words. They were enough. Almost.

"Well, when you remember, I shall take your call."

"Wh—"

She brought her fingers to her temple, "I do believe I forgot that a small megrim has settled in. Please excuse me." She turned to leave the room, then threw a look over her shoulder. *"I apologize."*

🔥

OH, THAT CURSED woman. She apologized. The gel apologized, did she? She forgot. She forgot a megrim. Cursedest of all females. Of course she was lying. It was patently clear, yet he could do nothing about it. Unless of course he wanted to bury himself further in poor etiquette. Clearly she was a stickler for propriety. Or something.

And why hadn't he brought flowers? He couldn't remember exactly. He knew he should have sent flowers. It was etiquette. That was partly why it nettled him so much. She was right. He was in the wrong. And he hated being wrong, almost as much as he hated swallowing his pride. Again.

It was a simple act of neglect. He should have made the arrangements this morning before breakfast, but in his mind he knew he was going to pay her a call. His presence was surely superior to a bouquet.

Regardless, the gel wanted flowers, he would get her flowers. Tomorrow. He had had enough for one morning.

He would take lunch at White's and see if anyone was there.

As it turned out, Samuel, James, and Chris were all sharing a meal together.

He sank into the last open chair at their table and heaved a sigh.

"Trouble with the lady?" Samuel jested, palms facing and fingertips touching to make the shape of a mountain. As if to say he was on top of it, and Wesley was merely attempting to scramble up it.

"Nothing I can't handle." Wesley placed his hand on the wooden table and rubbed its surface.

"She's a feisty one. That's for sure." Chris brought his fork to his mouth, but the food didn't quite make it in.

"What? You know her that well to know she's feisty?" Wesley demanded.

Chris glanced around the table. "Lady Zenobia's sister? Of course I know her. I know all the sisters. Their whole family in fact." The food reached its target, and he chewed and swallowed. Under duress no less. "What?" he finally asked.

"You didn't think to mention anything last night?" Wesley managed to keep his face impassive.

"What? You needed my help to ask a lady to dance?" Chris

scoffed.

"No," Wesley eyed his friend, "I didn't need your help asking her to dance. But didn't you think it was pertinent to disclose your proximity to the family?"

"I did not. The bet is between you and Samuel." Chris continued chewing. Annoyingly so.

"You're telling me that you don't remember the kissing bet we made on Chris and Zenobia?" Samuel jumped into the conversation.

Mouth full, Chris piped up, "We don't need to bring that up."

"Because you defaulted?"

"I didn't default."

"Did you kiss her?" Samuel prodded.

Chris crunched down on his food. "Whatever."

"Well, who won the bet?" James asked.

"I did," Samuel boasted.

"Of course, you did," Wesley wanted to revert the conversation back to Chris and Boudicca. "Would you say you're good friends with Boudicca?"

"We're friends. What do you want from me? We used to play together as children. I know she's feisty. I know she likes to fence. I don't know her favorite ice flavor or what music she likes."

"I get it. You're friends." Wesley put his hands up in defense.

This was not good. The exasperating woman was a friend. Well, a friend of a friend. He didn't want to do anything to jeopardize her reputation. Even more so now. And, perhaps for the first time, he appreciated the fact that he also didn't want to play around with her emotions at all. Not that he currently thought she had more than two: disdain and offense.

"Samuel—"

"Aha! Another attempt to weasel your way out of this bet."

"James—"

"This is between you and Samuel." James' hands were in the air. "You two made the ridiculous bet, now you can lie in it."

"Good one," Wesley said dryly.

"Don't be mad at me when you're the idiot." James chuckled.

"Right. I can see you three are going to be a great help in all of this."

"Happy to help." James slapped him on the shoulder.

"What kind of trouble did she give you?" Chris asked guilelessly.

"No trouble," he bit off. "I forgot to bring her flowers when I paid her a call today."

And that sent the three into wallops of laughter.

"Wesley," James shouted. "Are you new? Is this your first visit? What were you thinking ol' boy?"

"Apparently I wasn't."

"It sounds like you've met your match. There might be a lady out there with higher standards than you." Chris' chuckles subsided. "You better be ready to bring your best game, Wes."

"Yes. Well, I won't be caught unprepared again."

If only that were true, Wesley might have had more success the next day. The meal complete, a game of piquet won, Wesley was feeling on top of his game. It was a restful evening at home and a good long sleep. He had made arrangements for flowers to be delivered to his house the next morning, thus being able to present them in person. Nothing could top hand-delivered flowers.

Those thoughts should have lent to a peaceful sleep. But instead of a deep sleep, he dreamed of peonies. Pink peonies. Not red. Not white. No other colors at all. Just a pale pink flower with soft petals and a deep fragrance. He could almost smell it in his dream. That was a first. Dreams had the potential to be a safe place. A place where no harm could reach a person. A place where one could control everything. Add what they liked, discard what they didn't. Yet dreams rarely achieved their full potential. So, of course, when he reached out to touch the rose it had thorns. And the thorns were sharp. But it wasn't a sensation of pain that rattled through him. It was a sense of something else. Impossible to put into words, especially when one was dreaming.

And more especially because when one woke up, all one remembered was the pale pink peony.

Peonies, of all things.

CHAPTER FIVE

BOUDICCA SPENT THE morning reassuring herself that she, in fact, did not need to prepare for a second visit from the duke. She could, in reasonably good conscience, tell her sisters that she had snagged a duke, alas, he had gotten away. He was a slippery one, that silky-haired, steely-eyed duke with the strong, warm hands. A tingle crawled up her spine.

It had been far too long since a man had given her any masculine attention. She hadn't flirted in...ages. Not that she was the flirting type. Yet she felt a rather uncanny urge to stay on her toes. But that wasn't flirting.

When the butler came to announce a visitor, she knew it was the duke. What she didn't know was how to accurately label the energy coursing through her body. And that heated blood pumping through her veins...she wasn't quite sure what that was all about. Except, he had better have brought flowers this time. She would feel foolish claiming another megrim. By God, she would do it...but she would feel foolish.

Didn't she have a right to have high standards? Some women waited until they were seventy before they asserted themselves and opined on every subject. Boudicca was not waiting until seventy. She had lived through enough of the Marriage Mart to hold sky-high standards, and she wasn't about to drop them for anyone. Not even a duke.

If she was going to marry and compromise her plans of being

a foil-wielding spinster, then it had damn well better be worth the compromise.

So yes, the man needed to prove his mettle.

Confident in her resolve, Boudicca made her way to the drawing room. But with each step she took, the tingling along her spine grew. The correlation between the decreasing distance and the increasing tingles was irrefutable. This was almost akin to...nerves. How very odd.

This, she needed to understand more.

In front of the closed drawing room door she paused and rallied herself one last time. *Be yourself. Keep your standards high. Submit to no man. Trust no man. Be on your guard. Better yet, put him on his guard.* Ah...there it was. She breathed in and exhaled some excess energy.

Entering the room, she noticed that the duke had again been standing dead center in the middle of the room. This time though, he had a small smirk on his face. The smirk of a man with ulterior motives, to be sure. If she had had feathers, they would already be ruffled.

"Good morning, Your Grace." She drew out a curtsy, delaying the inevitable glance up at his face. When she finally did raise her head to meet his gaze, her breath caught in her throat. Damn his warm eyes, so at odds with his stony cold demeanor.

"It is lovely. I hope you've recovered from yesterday."

"Yesterday?"

Another smirk. "Your megrim."

"Of course..." How could she have been caught off guard already? But those eyes of his. They were peering into her. If his eyes were feet they would have been standing en garde in the shape of an L. She dropped her gaze to his feet. No L. Just shoulder width apart. And then, regarding the status of her megrim, she responded, "Well, that is yet to be seen."

He belted a short laugh. "I do hope it remains at bay."

She didn't want to hear his laugh. And she really didn't want to continue staring at his angular face that had a smooth cut jaw, which she was quite sure had stubble on it at the dance. Why she recalled that, and how it did something to her insides vexed her immeasurably.

So she flicked her eyes down his body instead. And she observed his hands. Large, smooth hands clasped in front of him. She didn't look further down, not much further anyway, as she could already feel a warmth creeping into her face. Her eyes began to steal their way back up his body, across those hands again. And that's when she noticed it. Empty.

His hands were empty. No flowers? Botheration. What did the man think of her? That she forgot? That she would reconsider her requirement to visit with him? The man was galling.

He cleared his throat. "Perchance, are you looking for these?" He stepped to the side and behind him, on the table were—not one, but two—bouquets of flowers. One bouquet of various flowers and—heaven above—one bouquet of pale pink peonies.

She gasped.

Her feet lost their place, even though they were standing still. The world had surely shifted. How had he known? What the deuce kind of sign was this?

It was not a sign she was ready or willing to concede, that's what kind of sign it was. He was an arrogant arse. A man far too high in the instep for her. Selfish. Greedy. Lavish. Deceitful. Though she knew none of these things to be true, she had to tell herself this. The alternative was too overwhelming. He couldn't possibly know her and be interested in her.

"May we visit this morning?" His tone was silky. And...amused. How infuriating! He knew the effect of the flowers, though maybe not the full extent of it.

No, she would most certainly not visit with this man. He was dangerous. In ways she could not fully understand. So she made a point to keep looking around the room.

She walked over to the flowers. Even sniffed the fragrant peonies. Her favorite. She couldn't resist. Also, she had to make a show of it, else she would lose her nerve.

"Lovely," she murmured. Then, standing to her full height, and looking him dead in the eyes, she asked, "Did you not bring me chocolates?"

CHOCOLATES?! UP UNTIL that point, he had her eating out of his hand. The visit was going to happen. He knew it. He felt it. He could sense it in his very being. But all that really meant was that he willed it. And he couldn't really perceive anything beyond his will. If he wanted it desperately enough, then nothing could stand in his way. Not fate. Not dreams. And especially not a mercurial old spinster.

When she had walked into the room, he had felt her restlessness. When he had stepped to the side, exposing the flowers, he felt that restlessness explode. And then her gasp had sealed it. He knew she loved them. They meant something more to her that he didn't understand. And he had been thanking his dream for the hint. He wouldn't have picked up the second bouquet that morning if it hadn't been for the dream.

The flowers had been divined. There was no other explanation. Her response, on the other hand, was infernal.

He had brought flowers. And on all accounts, he had chosen the perfect bouquet. Her eyes had lit up. Her cheeks had drawn in as her lips formed the perfect circle. If he didn't know better, he would have thought he had picked her favorite flower. By chance. And if she was a woman that he was keen on, he would have done some digging to confirm that fact, as he was not one to rely on capricious things like dreams to lead his love life. She was not a woman he was pursuing for love, or even lust (that motivation triggered all kinds of effort from him).

And now the cursed chit wanted chocolates, as well? Unheard of. He hadn't brought flowers, chocolates, and gifts all to any one woman. Flowers, here. Chocolates, there. The odd gift here and there (to a mistress or two), but never all at once to one lady. Who did she think she was?

But he had to tamp down his emotions. He needed to win this bet. Besting Samuel to prove that he was not a better judge of Wesley's love life was paramount. If there was a bullseye somewhere representing this bet, Samuel's smirking face was in the middle of it. So, although it was well within his prerogative to stand his ground against Boudicca, he wouldn't win his bet by ranting at her. Though he might have to plunge forward through gritted teeth.

"Chocolates? Oh?"

And she had the nerve to remain silent.

His tone belied his internal stewings. "I didn't realize that chocolates were a requirement."

She merely nodded.

"So," he pointed to the flowers, counting them in the air, "flowers are required. And...chocolates?" He drew out the sentence, just in case she wanted to interrupt him. She didn't.

"Yes, of course they are." She flicked her clear blue eyes up at him; a wisp of hair hung loosely against her jaw. He had the urge to tuck it behind her ear. Perhaps graze her cheek along the way. The urge was patently ridiculous.

"So, no visit today, I take it?"

And in a voice that he didn't predict, she squeaked out, "Certainly not." She cleared something, or nothing, from her throat. "It wouldn't be proper."

Proper? Hang it all. What this woman thought was proper was nothing more than her own ruminations. There was nothing proper about these requests. Let alone the fact that they were alone on both of the occasions he had visited. He hadn't heard any gossip involving any scandal with her, but perhaps there was a reason for her being a spinster. It might all be making significantly more sense right now. Thinking of her requirements for a visit...it was laughable. Or it should have been, except it was exasperating.

"All right then," he took a few strides toward the door, and he could hear her footsteps following close behind him. Likely to close the door on his behind.

Abruptly at the doorway, he stopped. She plowed right into him. Her head must have been down. But that wasn't his first thought. His first thought was about her hands that had fumbled on his hips to steady herself. Followed closely by a second thought regarding the feel of her breasts pressed into his back. He would have admitted that he liked the feel of her hands on his hips and her breasts against his back, but he didn't give himself time to evaluate the sensations.

Instead, he turned slowly. A slight blush had crept into her cheeks. Her hair should give up on the coiffure at this point. He leaned back and put one hand almost all the way up the doorframe. She was nearly tucked underneath him. If he was not irked just so, he might have felt...aroused. Towering over her he could picture his body covering her while she was strewn across his bed, subject to his every whim. But that had nothing to do with the bet. He narrowed his eyes at her, and battling his ducal proclivities, he maintained inquisitive rather than imperious eyebrows.

"Just to be sure, *when* I come back tomorrow. For a visit. With tea." He felt compelled to clarify at least a couple of terms. "I shall bring flowers and chocolates."

She nodded. Clear eyes with long lashes that she could have used to flutter at him, but didn't. No, she was not communicating coquettishly. Rather, she was direct. Said what she wanted. Didn't equivocate. Didn't back down. It was almost respectable, if the vexatious aspect didn't win out.

"Anything else?" he intoned.

"I'm sure you know which kinds of gifts are appropriate to give to a woman." She was giving him a tip. Something that he could prepare for rather than react to. He made a note to himself that progress was being made with her, albeit in the most roundabout fashion.

"A gift?"

Her nod caused a few more blonde wisps to come loose. They were baiting him.

"Flowers. Chocolate. *And* a small gift." He waited, watching her eyes, trying to read them, but they were closed off. "And then we shall visit?"

"Of course, Your Grace." She said the words as if it were ridiculous that she should have to clarify these obscure requirements. For to be sure, they were the obscurest he had heard yet. And he had many experiences from which to draw upon

"Fine. I shall see you tomorrow." And he almost bent down to press a kiss to her temple. It was right there. Would that kiss have been perfunctory or a means to throw her off whatever game she was playing, he didn't know. Thus he refrained.

As he pressed past her, he couldn't help but notice the lingering scent of roses like a cloud following him out the door.

Chapter Six

WHY, OH WHY, had she been staring at his buttocks?? If she had just been paying attention, she wouldn't have run right into him. Him and his strong, muscular back. She looked and felt a complete and utter bacon-brained ninny.

She thought she was going to lose it when she asked about the chocolates. And when she added the part about the gift, she couldn't even conceive of how she had abstained from laughter. It was all too much. And that's rather why she thought she was able to hold it all together. It *was* all too much. Him. His dukeness. His visits.

Tomorrow when he came, she would just outright decline his attention. That should do it.

But then tomorrow came. And so did he. With flowers. With chocolates. And with a small wrapped gift.

What ground did she have to stand on and refuse his attention? Pretty shaky, even she had to admit.

"Good morning, Lady Boudicca." He presented the flowers and a second bouquet of pale pink peonies. He had obviously appreciated her reaction yesterday.

She plucked a delectable looking chocolate from the small box sitting atop the gift. Heavenly. A moan nearly escaped her lips.

"That good, are they?"

Drat! Well, what could she expect? She wasn't chipped out of stone like he was.

She shrugged an indifferent shoulder. "Try one for yourself." But really hoping he wouldn't.

"I shall. Good to know you aren't one of those selfish recipients of gifts." He plopped one in his mouth.

"Yes, well. I pride myself on my virtues."

"Seems a contradiction, doesn't it?"

"Is it better to hold myself in contempt for my virtues?"

"Touché." The dratted man plopped another one of her chocolates in his mouth. "Shall we go for a carriage ride?"

"I thought you wanted a visit with tea?"

"I thought I did as well. And then I thought perhaps it's best we're in neutral territory where I can't be kicked out."

She hummed her deliberation. "While your carriage is most definitely not neutral territory, I can accept your offer if only to take some time outdoors."

"That's reason enough for me. Shall we?" He propped his arm up for her, and she took it. After having gone only a few steps, his feet melded into the Aubusson rug. "I nearly forgot your gift." Turning, still with her hand on his arm, he reached for the gift and tugged on the wrapping.

"Isn't it customary for the recipient to open their own gifts?"

"Isn't it customary...now that is quite the phrase. Shall we delve into that one?" The shape of his autocratic eyebrow curtailed her initial response.

"Just open it. You've already started." Her hand was still on his arm, and she could feel her breast rubbing against his forearm as he untied the last string.

There in dusty blue, laced in gold text, read, *Boudicca, A Warrior Queen Biography*.

"Charming," she murmured as she accepted the tome.

"I took the liberty of placing a few bookmarks next to my favorite quotes."

"You read this already?"

"Select parts."

With nothing to say to that, she stuffed the small book in her dress pocket and led them out of the house.

This man was vexing indeed. Soon it would be time to dig.

While it was one thing to be alone together in the privacy of her own home, it was another beast entirely to attempt that in public. It was a beast she declined to fight. A quick call to her lady's maid presented the perfect chaperone, and they were off, seated in the carriage and heading toward Rotten Row. With the knowledge that her questioning him would put a damper on the day, Boudicca allowed herself to enjoy the wind and the sun in companionable silence.

"I can see that smile. You should have let me take you on a carriage ride on my first visit."

"That is a thought. However, I would be out flowers, chocolates, and a nice little book."

He chuckled. A nice deep rumble from his chest. It was a contagious laugh that rendered her lips weak. A tepid smile ensued.

"Yes, well, we can't have that."

"I half expected us to be in a high-flying phaeton. You're a duke after all."

"Not my style. I prefer this stable and well balanced curricle."

Interesting. That choice rather matched the man she was coming to know. Whether she wanted to know him or not.

Boudicca scanned the park. Despite knowing they were here to be seen, she equally wanted to observe everything around her. Some women were walking casually with friends and family, while others were dressed in deceivingly expensive gowns in hopes of discreetly garnering attention from someone of the male variety. The same way a woman's clothing reflected her values and personality, a man's choice of transportation conveyed his true self.

As they continued to make their way through the park, Boudicca snuck a peek at the duke from the corner of her eyes. His build was long and full. Broad shoulders, no padding in his jackets. And he had a classic look, with dark blues and creams. No one could claim an ounce of ostentatiousness about him. If he wasn't as haughty as he was, she might admit that a natural attraction could develop. Then again, his stone cold mien was a bit off-putting.

At that moment, she noticed a flicker in the stone. As if it could grow any tighter...yet it did. Something minute, perhaps another person wouldn't have recognized it in him. It was a strange feeling indeed to take note of it herself. How she could read him to any degree was befuddling.

All the same, it was there. A colder coldness. When Boudicca followed his gaze, she saw the source of his reaction.

A gorgeous, slim, brunette—Lady Simone, if Boudicca recalled—was in an open carriage heading toward them. They were about to cross paths. It was a curious point that the duke would be steeling himself for such an encounter. True, she was a beautiful—

"—talker."

Boudicca blinked her eyes, startled that he had been speaking to her and she hadn't noticed.

"Talker?"

He flicked his eyes toward the dowager. "She's the kind that likes to talk."

Affronted for the female gender, Boudicca raised her brows. "And the affinity for conversation is something to disdain?"

"Only when it's an affinity for spreading falsehoods," he shot back.

She should have been paying more attention to his words than his body. What kind of woman was she becoming? Only around him, mind, but really, it was rather a nuisance to be so distracted.

"Well, yes. Of course, one should limit the gossip one partakes in."

"So I guess the word will be out this afternoon."

"The word?" She was feeling a bit simple, but it was better to ask and know than remain silent and pretend to know.

"The word that I'm courting you."

She sputtered, "You're courting me?"

"I'm sure I've done my part in making that obvious." He cast a glance at her over his shoulder. "The visits. Plural. The flowers. Plural. The chocolate and the gift. You must recognize the signs."

"I suppose the signs are there. But signs can have multiple interpretations." At times. She was pretty sure of the signs he was sending her, but it had been a while since she had been the recipient of such signs, and really, what was he all about? Her family was known for being eccentric. No one had courted her in ages. Why him? A handsome and powerful duke. And why now?

"Come now, you can't say you didn't know my intentions."

"I very well will say that I don't know your intentions. In fact, you bring up a very valid question. What are your intentions, precisely?"

He straightened his spine, and murmured, "It's not the time."

"What better time—"

"Good afternoon, Lady Simone," he called out. A bit early if Boudicca was being persnickety, which she was.

The slightly widened eyes of Lady Simone confirmed Boudicca's judgment. The duke was obviously avoiding her question. Well, he couldn't avoid it forever. She would see to that.

"Good afternoon, Your Grace."

"Lady Simone."

The ladies dipped their heads in acknowledgment of each other. Though it had to be noted that Lady Simone cast her a wary eye, which made Boudicca wonder what the lady knew of the duke. And how well she knew it exactly.

There was some small chatter, about a ball, or something. But at the mention of a fencing tournament, Boudicca's ears perked up.

"Will you and the Duke of Cadmore be joining the upcoming fencing tournament again?"

"Of course." The subtle movement of the duke's jaw tensing

caught her eye.

"Best of luck to you. *This* time." It was a clear mocking tone. And as if it were a side note, she added, "See you at the garden party later this week, Lady Boudicca."

He grunted, dipped his head and flicked the reins.

"I didn't realize you fenced?" Boudicca inquired. This line of conversation was of great interest to her.

Through clenched teeth, he said, "Yes, I do."

"Are you any good?" And really, it wasn't meant to be challenging, or mocking, or anything. It was a simple, direct question.

"You obviously heard that I lost the last tournament."

"Actually, I did not hear of that." Though she wasn't sure how she hadn't heard of it. She always tried to keep apprised of all fencing-related news amongst the *ton*.

And then there wasn't time to clear up the misperception that she wasn't taunting him because another carriage was rolling toward them. The dowager Duchess of Melson (who should really just be referred to as The Meddler, or maybe Meddling Melson) was soon upon them.

"Good day to you, Duke." Her brows were already waggling, and her lip was curled into a smile. "Lady Boudicca."

"And you, Madame."

Boudicca smiled in return.

"What fine company to find you in. I hadn't realized you two were acquainted. I've known Lady Boudicca since she was just a young girl. I'm glad to finally see her in worthy…amity." She winked. It wasn't discreet in the least. But for whatever reason, it caused Boudicca to grow increasingly aware of the man beside her. The one apparently courting her. The one she didn't trust was courting her. Yet, the one who was a hot-blooded, stone-cut of a man quite nearly touching her thigh, now that she thought about it. She scooted away from the fire. The hot-blooded stone. Or whatever he was.

"Yes, he's a good friend." Realizing the vague definition of *good friend*, she hurried to clarify. "Not a close friend. But a good man—person. He's...erm...nice. Enough." Botheration! Never, ever in her life had she stuttered so. What the deuce had come over her?

A gentle chuckle rumbled beside her. "Yes, well, thank you for that, Lady Boudicca." He turned to The Meddler. "It does her justice to have someone speak to her long standing character."

"I can't say enough about her. Do you know about her love for fen—"

"Oh, I nearly forgot the time. Apologies, Your Grace, but I have to return home." There was no chance that Boudicca wanted the duke to know her secret love of fencing. Not yet, at least. The duchess, though a meddler, was not a gossip. The two dominating roles in the *ton* were quite distinct. To Boudicca's knowledge, the duchess had kept the daughters' secrets to herself. So it was unexpected that she was about to spill the tea now. And not even over tea.

It was time to leave. Thankfully, the duchess was already waving her goodbye.

"I think that was enough of a carriage ride for one day, don't you, Your Grace?" Boudicca smoothed her skirts and picked a few flecks of fluff from her sleeves. Surely she needed to get out of the warm summer sun before freckles sprouted. Not that she cared about that, but any excuse for space from the duke would do right about now.

"A gossip and a meddler both in one day compels me to agree with your evaluation." He turned the horses to head back to her house.

Despite a faint sense of a sinking in her shoulders, she was relieved. Quite relieved, she confirmed to herself.

"I shall call on you tomorrow then. We'll go for ices."

"Typical," she muttered. Did he think that just because he was a duke that he could call on her any old time that he wanted and that she would just have to accept his call? Well, yes, that was the way of society. So yes, she expected she would accept his call. Again.

Ices didn't seem so bad. If it weren't for the fact that it was all just so typical. A home visit. A carriage ride. Ices. It's what every courting couple did. Boudicca assumed that if one day she were to ever find a love match, it wouldn't be so deuced typical. If she were to ever accept that a man was truly interested in her for herself, he would have to be different than the other men that had courted her. She would have a sense of who he was, before he even told her. And he would somehow know things about her as well.

Caught in her ruminations yet again, Boudicca started when the carriage lurched to a stop in front of her house. She would see him tomorrow. For ices. Well, for that, she was already forming a plan in her mind. So it would likely not be typical at all tomorrow.

And then he had to go and say something that almost made her rethink her scheming.

"Just for the record, I find you nice…enough…as well."

CHAPTER SEVEN

EARLY AFTERNOON THE next day, Boudicca sat in the drawing room ready and waiting for the duke. It couldn't be helped. She was actually…could she admit it…excited for the outing. Oh, not because of the duke himself per se. More so, she was anticipating her little ploy for the day. Her fingers were restless, smoothing her skirts for the fifteenth time. Make that fourteen and a half, she refused to let her nerves get the best of her, so she stopped mid-smoothing halfway down her thighs. There was nothing to smooth anyway.

But the anticipation was wreaking havoc on her calves. She couldn't stop her heels from bouncing on the ground. Up and down and up and down. This was a perfect way to lose weight, should one want to shed a stone or two.

Finally, the knock on the door came. The butler was swinging open the door and Boudicca was at his side.

"Thank you, Arnolds. I'll take it from here."

Before the duke could even open his mouth to utter the expected morning salutation, Boudicca grabbed his arm. "No time to dally." Though no dallying was being done.

"I wouldn't imagine dallying with you." She could feel his eyes boring into the side of her head while she pondered the meaning behind what he had just said.

Choosing to give him the benefit of the doubt, though not entirely sure why, she replied, "Wonderful. Then we won't waste any time."

"I have to ask. Is your appetite for ices always this strong?"

He couldn't have asked a better question to set her up for her scheme if she had provided the question for him. With a wide grin on her face, not plastered at all, quite natural in fact, she simply said, "Always."

He chuckled as he helped her up into the carriage.

It was a short ride to Gunter's at Berkley Square and an even shorter wait to put in their order. It was the moment Boudicca was most looking forward to. It was the moment she had lost sleep over the previous night. And it was the moment in which she hoped to finally shake the duke from her hem.

They were sitting at their round table with a small flower arrangement between them. A lace tablecloth lay atop cream linen with a cloth napkin.

It was all quite lovely and proper, so when the confectioner asked, "Which flavor would you like, my lady?"

It was glaringly improper for Boudicca to reply, "All of them."

Taken aback, the man prompted, "We have white coffee, lavender, elderflower, brown bread, pistachio, parmesan, coriander, cinnamon, and artichoke."

"Sounds delicious." She smiled up at the balding man who now had a very curious look on his face.

He darted a glance at the duke. Then back to her. Then back at the duke. After deciding to land back on her, because really, he wanted a clear answer, he asked again, "Which one?"

"All of them, thank you." She dropped her head, mostly to prevent herself from releasing the chuckle that was lodged in her throat.

A throat cleared. "But which—

The duke interrupted. "All eight will do."

"There are nine."

"Even better," the duke bandied. "Bring us all nine flavors of ice."

Her head still bowed, she couldn't observe his reaction.

"I see you weren't misleading me when you attempted to prepare me regarding your appetite for ices."

Finally, she looked up. She knew a smirk was troubling the corner of her mouth, but she played it off. "I do love a good treat." She felt a little twinge of guilt knowing the exorbitant cost of the desserts and knowing full well that they wouldn't eat them all, but she pushed it aside. "And since I don't frequent Gunter's often enough, I thought it would be best to maximize my time here."

"They're all for you, then?"

"Of course, you thought I'd share?"

"I…"

She couldn't hold in the chuckle. "Of course, I'll allow you a couple of bites."

"A couple of bites or a couple of bowls?"

"We shall see," she said archly. "I do hope at least one of them comes in the shape of a bird. Preferably a hummingbird. I just love their dag—darling beaks." She almost said that she loved their dagger-like beaks.

"The last time I was here I received my chocolate ice in the shape of a lion."

"You say that with some pride," she said slyly. "Do you think that they match the animals to the patrons, Your Grace?" Boudicca cast a furtive glance around the room, taking note of anyone with a freshly served ice in front of them.

"Just Wesley."

"Where is he seated?"

"No," he chuckled, "you can simply call me Wesley now. May I call you Boudicca?"

The distraction to keep her eyes roaming the room hopefully hid a small blush crawling up her neck. It felt too intimate to call him Wesley, and to allow him to call her by her Christian name. But something inside her revolted against her pride and charged toward familiarity. It would be nice to be on a first name basis with the duke—Wesley. The name meandered through her mind, and her lips puckered softly at the thought of sounding it out.

"Yes, that's fine," she quipped. To regain her equilibrium, she focused on something shallow, "What about my question, though?"

"Ah…let me see," Wesley leaned forward unnecessarily, arms on the table, hands closer to her own. She dare not move for fear of advancing rather than retreating. There was a magnetism about him. Something she wanted to understand. It was his ulterior motives, she kept telling herself. But his scent of sandalwood wafting over her blurred her thoughts.

"Well, unless you know something about our dear old, wrinkly Lord Grimsley that I don't, I'd say the ices do not reflect the customer."

Boudicca grew giddy at the game they had started to play. "Oh really? Do tell, what shape is before him?"

"I cannot say. You must take a look for yourself." He grinned.

"I can't look now. He'll know we're talking about him." How she wanted to turn her head and look, but she also didn't want to embarrass the kind man.

"You can look. No one's watching us."

"I can't," she almost squealed, feeling the embarrassment for herself.

But then he dropped the gauntlet. "I dare you."

She just stared at him.

Did he know about her sisters and their dares? How had he found out? The only people to know of the dare were the four sisters. Surely, they hadn't been overheard. And without question, none of the four would have let their secret dare slip. Oh, how mortified she would be if Wesley found out about the dare.

As she studied his face, there was no guile. It was just a silly tease. But one she was not going to pass up.

She tilted her body forward and whispered, "All right. I'll look." Dropping her shoulder, she peered behind her at Lord

Grimsley's table. There in front of the hunched over old man with a round face and no hair was the shape of his ice: a wolf.

She casually turned her head back to Wesley and gave him a full smile. "I dare say you are correct. The shape is arbitrary."

And just as she finished saying that, nine shapes were brought to their table. Among the nine, a bird was placed in front of Wesley. He pushed it toward her.

"I believe these are yours to distribute as you see fit."

She passed him a spoon. "Let's just enjoy them all together." With that, they dug into the treats, both grinning like small children.

"You seem to have a favorite," Boudicca said, motioning to the white coffee.

"Really? How can you tell?"

"Well, the white coffee used to be in the middle of the table, and for the past few minutes your spoon has hovered sentry over it."

Wesley belted a short laugh. "I've been caught." He took another bite. "It's sublime. I can't believe I've never had it before. That may have something to do with the fact that I only ever get one flavor when I visit Gunter's." After one more spoonful, he slid it back to the middle of the table. "Here, have some."

"It is delicious. Thank you, but it's all yours. My favorite is the pistachio."

After a few more bites, a shadow fell on the table.

"Wesley, good to see you." The deep voice held an almost mocking tone. Or perhaps it was more amused. They did have nine ices in front of them.

Wesley looked up slowly. "Samuel. Didn't know you would be here today."

He returned in jest, "Didn't get my weekly schedule again, did you?"

"Probably tucked away under my to-be-read files."

Samuel grinned. "Did you have lunch today?"

"Yes. Already come and gone just like every other day."

"I only ask because…" he swept his hand over the table.

Boudicca held her breath. She didn't know what she expected Wesley to say. He was a duke, so he would likely say something appropriate. Then again, it was a close friend that had issued the light challenge. Would he be the duke or the friend at this moment? Would transparency or propriety win out? He had options for what to say. *The lady loves ices. We were hungry. Gotta try 'em all. They're not mine.* She knew it was silly to have ordered all nine flavors, but she wasn't quite sure how silly it was.

But he just raised his spoon, saying, "This is for all those evenings when my mother limited us to only one flavor."

Samuel chuckled, tipped his head, and walked away.

It was a little bit adorable how Wesley had toasted her choice for all nine ices.

"Was your mother cruel or kind to limit your treats?" she found herself asking, wanting to know him just a little bit more.

"Always kind." He stuck his spoon into the white coffee hummingbird. "She was a loving mother. I have no complaints out of the ordinary."

"Just the ordinary complaints then. That consists of…?"

"Typical tantrum-worthy decisions. One flavor of ice," he nodded to the plates, "early bedtimes, no playing with weapons in the house." He laughed. "All wise decisions. What is your mother like?"

"She's passed on now."

"I'm sorry."

Boudicca could feel a sting of tears at her eyes, but she marshaled her emotions. "It was a few years ago now. It's all right." But he reached out to touch her hand anyway. It was…about the least he could do, especially publicly. But it's not as if she wanted him to do more. And it wasn't as if she were baring her soul. "It's fine." She forced her voice to perk up. "She was a wonderful mother. Sounds…similar to yours." Similar, but not quite the same. They had played with weapons inside. Many of them, in fact. But, she wasn't going to share that yet.

"Well, to good mothers then." He raised his spoon again. "May we appreciate their rules when they knew best and break them when we think we know better."

She chuckled as she lifted her full spoon in the air. "To mothers," she murmured.

It was at that moment that they both noticed Lord Grimsley making his exit. Just as the old man passed their table, they overheard him say to his companion, "Full moon tonight, isn't it?"

And then they buckled in laughter.

CHAPTER EIGHT

THAT EVENING, BOUDICCA ventured to The Practice Hall to release some pent up energy. She donned her fencing gear, complete with trousers, and began her exercises starting with the standing Y repeated twelve times. All the while she heard Wesley's laughter over the moon comment and saw his smile after trying the white coffee flavor for the first time. He was kind. And kind of adorable. And a little bit adoring. She wouldn't go so far as to say that it was genuine adoring, but…he had been willing to share his favorite ice. That said something about a person. He had also been willing to take the fall for ordering all the ices. That also said something. And then they had laughed together over such a silly joke about a wolf. Which also said something about him.

But with everything said about him, she still wasn't sure what she really knew about him.

The door opened, and in walked her three sisters. It was more common than not for the four sisters to practice at the same time, though they all worked on their individual skills. And often they would spar with each other, for there were no other ladies of the *haute ton* they had brought into their coterie.

This evening it seemed as though all the sisters were interested in fencing. Rapiers clicked and clanged and within the hour, the two pairs were past perspiring and were full blown sweating through their gear. No wonder society deemed that this was not an activity for ladies.

Boudicca stopped to grab some water after winning the rounds against each sister. Fencing was her forte after all. She took a glass and poured some water, flanked by her sisters.

"So..."—Mimi gulped some water down—"Are you going to share what you've been up to the past few days, Bodi?"

Of course her sisters would pounce on her the first chance they got. She was surprised they hadn't cornered her earlier. Almost four days had passed since the dare had been issued.

"I've been out."

"We know," Mimi intoned, hands on hips. "Do you think we'd be the last to find out? You know we live here, right? We're aware the duke has visited. Multiple times."

"Hmmm..." Boudicca stalled.

"Were you going to share with us, Bodi?" Joan asked quietly.

"We're here for you if you want to talk," Nobi chimed in now, too. "We'd like to know what's going on. Four visits in four days...What's he like? Does he make you laugh? Do you think he's handsome?"

"I'd like to know what's going on, too," Boudicca confessed. "I don't understand him."

"He's courting you," Mimi announced.

"Yes...I realize that...but, I don't know *why* he's courting me."

"You're kind, intelligent, beautiful—"

"Possibly. But he doesn't know that." Boudicca had to interrupt.

"He must. He has eyes," Mimi retorted. "Deep, brooding eyes..."

"Deep and brooding? Really Mimi?" Nobi tapped her rapier against her boot.

"If you haven't noticed his eyes, you're either deceiving yourself or you haven't opened yours." Mimi jabbed her finger into Nobi's shoulder a couple of times as if to wake her up.

"It isn't worth arguing over. His eyes are deep,

and…brooding—"

"So you think he's handsome then?"

Boudicca sighed. "Also not worth arguing over. It's quite an obvious fact that Wesley is a handsome man."

The sisters gasped collectively, which led to some giggles.

"What?" Boudicca defended herself when she shouldn't have had to. "He is handsome. Why would I be contrary and say otherwise."

"You called him Wes-ley," Mimi sing-songed. "Wes-ley and Bo-di."

"How childish, Mimi. Really." Boudicca tightened her lips, but Mimi didn't stop her singing.

"Wes-ley and Bo-di. Wes-ley and Bo-di."

Nobi spoke over the immaturity. "Has he caused any floating feelings, loose limbs, fluttery heartbeat, or bouncy steps in you?"

Boudicca rather thought Nobi was speaking from personal experience, given the specificity with which she asked about physical reactions. "It's been more sinking feelings, heavy limbs, erratic heartbeats, and dreaded steps."

"Well, that's…something at least?" She sounded hopeful.

Boudicca huffed. With her level of spinsterhood, she would likely never have physical reactions like that to a man. It was despairing, even though she thought she had already accepted her fate, there was some disappointment welling within her. And it was perhaps exasperated by Mimi's incessant taunting.

"Wes-ley and Bo-di."

"Mimi, do you want to know what's happened or not?" She practically stamped her foot at her youngest sister.

"Quiet, Mimi. We want to actually hear what's going on between Bodi and Wesley, not just hear your childishly melodic ode." With Joan and Nobi on her side, Mimi finally shut up.

"Right then. He's courting me. We've done what a typical courting couple would do." And she summarized the preceding days' events, only leaving out the trifling matters. Like her feelings on it all. "So that's that."

"Do you like him?" Joan asked.

"I don't know," Boudicca shrugged. "I can't take his courtship seriously. There must be an ulterior motive."

"He's not the enemy," Joan said gently.

"That's just it. He feels like the enemy."

"All the more reason to get to know him better," Nobi said, lifting a finger to the air. "Know your enemy and know yourself. You know, The Art of War and all."

"It's not a battlefield, Nobi," Joan said.

Mimi took a step back, en garde. "Love is always a battlefield." She swished her sword through the air.

Boudicca rolled her eyes. "Well, as silly as it sounds, it does feel like it's a battlefield."

"Then the only way you'll really know him is to show him who you really are," Joan crossed her arms. "But can you do that?"

"I've only been myself with him." Boudicca's tone sounded strained even to her own ears.

"Have you?" Joan was quiet, but she wouldn't back down from a challenge, especially when she knew she was right.

"I have."

"So he knows that you fence?" Joan countered.

"No."

"He knows about spinsterhood plans?"

"No."

"Fencing school for girls?"

"No."

"Interest in politics?"

"No."

"Favorite color?"

"I don't know."

"Bodi," Joan paused, "the man knows nothing about who you really are. You have to show him."

"I—I can't."

"Yes, you can," Joan urged.

It felt childish, weak, too vulnerable to tell her younger sisters why she couldn't open up to Wesley. Or any man, really. If she revealed herself to him and he rejected her, it would be too painful.

"It's terrifying to share your true self with someone." Nobi patted Boudicca's arm. "Especially when you feel you can't trust them. But I think it'll be worth it."

"So you agree with Joan?" Boudicca asked.

Joan and Nobi nodded.

"You know what you have to do, Bodi." Mimi wheeled around on her heel and swung her sword again. "You have to fence with him."

"What? Why?"

"You know why." Mimi stood still as a statue. "It's who you are. Show him who you are."

"I don't trust him. There's something else going on He has some kind of ulterior motive, so why would I make something real out of this when it's all fake?"

"Like begets like," Joan said. "Open up and he will too."

"Maybe…" Boudicca hesitated.

And Mimi swept in. "Then don't be too real. Be real enough to find out what it is. Or get your own ulterior motive. Then you'll be even."

"You mean besides the dare?"

Mimi waved her hand dismissively. "Of course, besides the dare. That's not an ulterior motive. That's a real motive. Get married to secure your future. There's nothing nefarious or surprising there. Put him on his guard. Attack him. Literally, and find out for yourself what he's up to."

"That's not a terrible idea…"

"THAT'S A TERRIBLE idea. I can't fence with you," so said Wesley the next morning when he came to visit. He had planned to visit this morning. Again. And the plan was to plan when he would propose. That was the plan. But the proposed plan was not unfolding. He couldn't think straight. Not only because she looked quite fetching in her sapphire blue frock (forget that thought), but also because she had greeted him with *Shall we try fencing today?*

Boudicca stood, indicating the hardly-started visit was coming to an end. With a long inhale, an inhale that caused a heave of her bosom which directly sent a flare to his groin, she said, "It was worth a shot to ask."

Etiquette dictated that Wesley stand when a lady did, so he was on his feet. Though his footing was slightly off balance after the heaving and the flaring. Hang it all. She wanted to fence with him...that had to be the oddest request he'd ever had from a lady.

"Why do you want to fence? I'm courting you. We should visit. Get to know each other." He hardly believed he had to convince her of the proper way to court a lady. But then again, this was the same lady who hadn't done anything conventionally yet. So really, he shouldn't be so foolish to think that she would start now.

Yet...yet, something had clicked into place over ices. He couldn't shake the feeling. What the feeling was, he wasn't sure. Comfort? Familiarity? Contentment? They had shared a few laughs and enjoyed their time. It had all the appearances of a typical day out. Save the nine animal-shaped ices strewn about the table. Amused at the thought, and delighted to have discovered a new favorite flavor, he couldn't cast any blame over her.

But fencing?

And while he had been ruminating, she had been retreating. He gave a last ditch effort of an excuse.

"I've nothing to wear."

Her eyes roamed his body from head to toe, and for some reason it made him puff out his chest. Just a touch. A slightly larger inhalation than perhaps would have been normal. And yes, he may have adjusted his shoulders by pulling them back. A hair. Not worth noting. Her gaze was a challenge he wasn't willing to lose.

"You want to get to know me, but you want to control everything about how you court me?"

"I want to control everything?" he gave her as dubious a stare as he dared. "I assure you, if I were the one in control—"

"No matter. You've made up your mind. And so I've made up mine."

She wasn't getting away that easily.

"Oh, we'll fence. But let the record show how adamantly I insisted that this was a terrible idea."

"The record will show. Have no fear." She turned toward the door, but not before he glimpsed a small smirk on her face. "I'll grab you some of my brother's gear. You're about the same size."

In fact, he was not the same size as her brother. He was slightly larger in every way, and he was pulling at the sleeves that rested a couple of inches above his wrists. And his trousers were…tight to say the least. Notwithstanding, his ankles seemed to enjoy the breeze. She had left him to change behind the screen in a large hall arena. Gymnasium clad with weapons. So…an armory of sorts? But the weapons were not on display. At least, they didn't look as though they were only on display. They looked used. Well-used.

Futilely, he tugged on his sleeve again. With a grunt, he bent down to adjust his trousers, then reconsidered how far he could bend. This would severely limit his movements if he wanted to maintain propriety. Cursed gel! He had already determined that he would play left-handed against her so as not to completely annihilate her. He was a man after all, and he had nearly won the last cursed fencing tournament against his cursed best friend, Samuel. Thankfully, he had not had a match against Lord Tamely. The man was a notorious cheat. And briber. He had seen the knave trip a man and claim a point while the referee turned a blind eye. Despicable, that. But there was no recourse for the call.

Infused with the ugly memory and uncomfortably clad, he waited for his enigmatic opponent.

Clearly, he was in great spirits at the prospect of parrying with Boudicca.

But even with the cringe-worthy fit of his gear, and the sensory onslaught of the unique armory-slash-gymnasium, he was altogether a complete slack-jawed mess when Boudicca entered the hall.

CHAPTER NINE

When Boudicca finally entered the Practice Hall, as she and her family members had come to call it, and met him on their equivalent of a piste, she should have realized it would be a shock to Wesley to see her in trousers. His gaping jaw was abruptly clamped shut, but she had momentarily seen the man's tonsils. It was an adorable reaction. His lingering gaze from toe to head was enough to make her blush. If she had allowed it. Instead, she shook his gaze, grabbed her rapier, and decided to spare conversation.

She wanted to see what he was made of. See if he changed at all when pushed, for she knew she was about to push him past his expectations. This was what she and her sisters had discussed. *Show yourself to him, and he'll be compelled to do the same.* That was the idea anyway.

Having fenced with very few men, her nerves were as frayed as the hem on a three year old frock. Worse. But she was not the kind to back down from a challenge. One need only reference her involvement in the asinine sororal dare. Botheration. Really, the best way through something was the direct approach.

No holds barred, Boudicca took her stance.

"En garde, Wesley."

"Prêts?" She watched as he passed his sword to his left hand. She wanted to growl her response to his question as to whether she was ready or not. Frayed nerves aflame, a new emotion was set ablaze in her. Absolute, pure fury. Without a doubt, she knew he was right-handed, for she had seen the man eat. Ostensibly, he felt his skills were far superior to her own if he was choosing to apply his weaker hand.

She hopped her blade to her left hand as well. There would be no mercy. "Allez," she thundered to start the bout.

And immediately she took the attack. Advancing with a lunge to the high outside. One. He parried and made a riposte. A passé, missing her completely. She feinted left, then struck low outside. Two. With a quick appel, her foot stomped the ground, temporarily distracting him. She struck low inside and pulled back. Three.

Her ears were thundering and her pulse was hammering through her. As if there were an attaque au fer, blade to blade, blood to limb assault in her own body, she could barely contain her rage. If eyes were blades, hers would steal another point, but she had already won. She retreated.

"That's three."

Clearly dazed, he was huffing.

Good. She pointed her rapier to his left hand. "Don't ever insult me like that again."

"I—"

"Again," she demanded, while striking her pose.

He flipped his blade to his dominant hand. When she did not mirror his actions, he tilted his head. But the commands had already been called.

She scored three to his two. By then she was having a little bit of fun.

"Again," she shouted, her blade flipped to her right hand. This time she would leave nothing on the mat. The duke could love her or hate her for it, but she would show him everything she had.

Advance-lunge. High inside. One.

Retreat. Advance. Feint. Low inside. Two.

Retreat. Retreat. He lunged. A passé. And then...

She wheeled her blade high, swung it over her shoulder and the tip of her blade swung under her arm and tapped him low inside. Three.

"What the deuce was that?" Wesley shouted, eyes wide, voice rumbling. He sounded more than a little angry.

"What was what?"

"That!" He attempted to duplicate her movements by swinging his rapier up and then crashing down on himself.

It was ambitious to hold in her laughter, but she succeeded. She was walking over to the water stand, which helped control her amusement. It was a quick second to pour herself a glass to drink, and a bit of a slower second to gulp it down. Normally not one to gulp down anything in the presence of a man, she threw etiquette out the window.

"Boudicca, what the bloody hell was that?"

"It's my signature move."

"How do you even have a signature move?"

"Practice."

"Practice? That's all you have to say in explanation?"

"Hours and hours of practice."

He waited.

"Upon years and years of practice." She poured another drink. "Is that a satisfactory explanation?"

He was shaking his head, almost as if he had water in his ears. "How in the world did you come up with that?"

"I thought I'd explained—"

He put up a hand. "I know. Practice." A whistle blew out between his lips. "I have never"—his eyes met hers—"in all *my* years of…practice, met anyone who has done anything remotely close to that maneuver."

"Thank you." And then she smiled. A triumphant smile if there ever was one.

"You have to teach me that."

And then she folded in laughter. No matter how many hours she spent with him, he wouldn't just be able to do it. She had never seen or heard of anyone who had done it. Her fencing master himself, even after years of fencing with her, had yet to be able to mimic it. And not for want of trying. Oh, the man had been eager to replicate it. But the eagerness had waned over the years. He still attempted it, but...it was one of her foolproof moves.

"Sure. I'll teach that to you right after you teach me to be a rake." Oh, why had she said that? She was not normally one prone to impulsive verbiage.

"Well, I guess I could—"

"Forget what I just said."

"All right—"

"I wasn't thinking."

"No matter. It's forgotten."

"Shall we go again?"

"I think not."

So that was that then. He had made up his mind about her. And he wasn't in it. She peeked up at him, as he hung the sword back in its place. He appeared rather out of it, if she were taking proper note of his body language.

"My pride has suffered enough blows for one day." He turned to face her again, and sighed. "However, now that I know your secret, my pride shan't take such a beating the next time we parry."

Her heart fluttered. He wanted to see her again. More than that, he wanted to fence with her again. Silly heart, be calm.

"You're assuming I'll want to fence with you again."

"Yes."

Well. It was true. And he had just called her bluff.

But her dignity...what of that? She needed it intact. "Tomorrow then. Ten. Don't be late."

AFTER WAKING UP on the couch the next morning, Wesley couldn't help thinking that that was the most intimidating, most glorious event he had ever witnessed in fencing. Perhaps in any sporting event. And by a woman! Most assuredly, she was living up to her namesake. She was a warrior. Bet aside (almost), he now just wanted to be near her to learn some fencing techniques he might employ on Samuel in the next tournament. He was in need of some fresh moves. That, and partly he wanted to see how she might next surprise him.

His father would have a heyday, seeing Wesley lose. And to a woman, at that. He could still hear his father's threat. *Don't come home unless you win. Losers don't sleep in this house.* And that had been drilled into Wesley's head almost from birth. And the first time he lost, a ridiculous footrace of some kind at his fifth birthday party, his father told him to sleep over at his friend's house. It hadn't been harsh. It was just a simple dismissal. He didn't want to look at him. And the first time it happened (the sleepover that is), Wesley was thrilled enough to spend more time with his friend. It was when the dismissals happened again and again, each time a little harsher, that Wesley felt the sting of them.

Losing to Boudicca had him torn. In one sense, it was a loss. It stung. Not that he would let her see that. But in another sense, he appreciated her skill and could see how he could exploit his time with her.

He was still in a state of shock by the time he arrived at her house the next day. Not a minute late. In fact, he was a few minutes early as he strode up her front steps, so he found his mind wondering, not for the first time, why no one was ever at home when he called. Boudicca had explained that given her age, her family had agreed to let her be. Wesley couldn't help thinking that she had probably just told them to let it be, and so they had. And just as he was thinking that, before he even knocked, Arnolds opened the door and he came face to face with three sisters coming down the stairs.

And then he thought, *why did I have to go and wonder about no one being home?*

The sisters were bantering amongst themselves when they stepped down into the foyer, and even though Arnolds had only taken his hat and coat, he felt a bit exposed.

"I'm here to see Boud—Lady Boudicca."

"Bodi's in The Practice Hall already, Your Grace," Lady Artemisia spoke up.

"Thank you. I'll be on my way then."

"So you know her secret then?" Lady Zenobia asked.

"Yes, we had a bout yesterday."

With some astonishment, Lady Artemisia asked, "And you came out unscathed?"

"If one's pride doesn't count."

"Touché." He was pretty sure Lady Joan uttered that single word, but he was trying to make his way toward the gymnasium, without being impudent.

"We shan't keep you from your visit."

And he had almost quit the room when Lady Artemisia tapped him on the arm and whispered, "But if you hurt her," and then she drew a line across her throat, smiled, and skipped away with her sisters.

Chills ran down his spine. If Boudicca had secrets, the other sisters might have as well. He recalled the various weapons in The Practice Hall, shuddering to think which weapon of choice belonged to Lady Artemisia. She was the youngest of the four, but perhaps the most reckless.

He arrived in the gymnasium and observed as Boudicca practiced her single leg hops. His focus on her thighs. Those thighs would probably have an incredible grip around his hips. He blasted the thought from his mind.

"I've brought my own gear today." He lifted his satchel in proof.

She ignored his words as she finished her exercises. Breathless, she called out to him. "You can change behind the screen again." She pointed it out to him as if he had forgotten about it since yesterday. "That's what it's there for."

It felt awkward this time to change in the room because she was in it. And she was close enough to him that he could hear her heavy breathing. And that heavy breathing was doing something to him that he wasn't ready to admit.

He ducked behind the screen and changed quickly, affording himself little time to dwell on the swelling member between his legs.

Fencing. Attacks. Parries. That's what he was here for.

When he emerged, his body and all its parts were in their restful proportions. He grabbed a foil from the wall and proceeded to the piste.

"I know you pronounced it an impossibility, but would you consider demonstrating your signature move all the same?"

Her smile and clear blue eyes stirred something within him. He had deemed her fetching in that sapphire blue from days ago, but in trousers, with a foil in her hand, she was a warrior he might follow into battle.

"Of course, Wesley."

And his name on her lips…heat seared his heart. What the deuce was that about?

Corralling his thoughts, he studied her movements. She was lightning quick, and he barely registered the whipping of the blade. When she repeated her movements, slower the second time, he forced his ears to listen to her describing the action.

"You try." She motioned for him to stand in front of her.

When he attempted the move, halfway through the swing, his body drew a blank on what came next.

"From here, what's next?"

He expected her to vocalize the subsequent action, so when she didn't say anything, he forced his body to complete the arc it had started.

A soft grunt sounded close to his ear. He hadn't seen her come up behind him and his blade made contact with her.

He whirled around. "I didn't know you were—Oh my God, Boudicca, you're bleeding."

Her hand was on her neck.

"What happened?" His eyes dropped to his blade.

"I didn't see that you grabbed the wrong sword."

"You have unprotected swords in here?"

"Yes." Nonplussed, he watched as she walked over to the water station and grabbed a small cloth.

"Hang it all. You're bleeding. I stabbed you."

"You didn't stab me."

"What do you call it when a blade makes contact with skin and draws blood?"

"I walked into it. It's my fault." She was pressing the cloth against her neck.

"Sit down." He looked around, but there were no chairs. "Just sit on the floor. Let me see the damage."

"No damage. I've had worse."

"Just sit down, will you?"

Together they sat on the floor, leaning their backs against the wall. He took the cloth from her hands, and brushed a few strands away from her neck. He could feel the heat from her body, and his breathing was labored. Even though he was the uninjured party. "Let me see," his voice was a hoarse whisper.

Her body was rigid, and he saw how she twitched when his fingers grazed her soft skin. Just this small, soft touch lay siege on his warrior queen's defenses.

"You act as if you've never been this close to a man before?" Surely she had stolen a few kisses in her years. She was a beautiful woman after all, at least one man must have pressed his lips to her crimson petals.

But her whispered reply shattered his illusions. "I haven't."

CHAPTER TEN

SHE SHOULDN'T HAVE disclosed that fact. Obviously, he surmised, for absolutely no reason other than perhaps she was a forward-thinking woman for having the secret skill of fencing, that she was a forward moving woman in other areas as well. Well, she wasn't. And it was no more painfully clear to her than at this moment, with his soft, warm breath against her neck, and his soft, warm fingers stroking her ear, that she had not ever been in such close quarters with a man. Let alone such a gorgeous specimen of a man.

Why had she exposed herself to him? It was bad enough the cut was stinging, she didn't need her heart and her pride stinging as well.

But the words were out there.

And his look of shock, quickly covered in a cool demeanor, had her heart rate pulsing. What was he going to do with his newfound knowledge?

"Never?" he whispered, another stroke along her ear.

"What kind of woman do you take me for, Duke?" The tone she was going for was umbrage, but the execution sounded much more strained.

"You know…I'm not quite so sure anymore." He was leaning toward her. His lips were inches from her face.

This was not how she had imagined her first kiss. She could feel control slipping from her fingers. And if she lost her grip on it completely, she wasn't exactly sure where her fingers would end up. His dark, silky locks. His rippling bicep covered in a mere thin layer of linen. His sharp jaw. There were so many places to explore. So many manly places she had denied herself. Even in her imagination. She was a spinster. She was going to open a fencing school for girls. She had plans. But right now, those plans were being threatened by parted, lush lips.

And more importantly, she was not impulsive. Especially when being impulsive meant jumping into something she wasn't confident in. If she was going to do something in the spur of the moment, it would be something she knew she was good at. And, sadly, kissing wasn't one of those skills. Having never done it. There was no way she was going to show that level of vulnerability to Wesley.

"I'm fine," her voice struggled for clarity. But at least it had accomplished its objective. The leaning stilled.

She brushed his hand off of her neck and checked the cut.

"You're still bleeding."

"It's just a scratch. I'm fine. Did you come here to fence or not? A moment more, and I'll question your motives, sir." What she meant was that she would question them a whole lot more than she already did.

She stood and marched over to the piste, holding her blade high. But it wasn't the same as yesterday. Yesterday had been full of anticipation and eagerness. There was a thrill in the air. Today the thrill was replaced by a chill.

Whatever heat had been simmering between them as they sat on the floor together had grown cold.

And she knew she wasn't alone in feeling tense. Truth be told, it was not a good state to be in when engaging in combat, even a friendly one.

The blades met, and from the first clang, she knew this way led to trouble. It was a harbinger of dread to heed.

She lunged, attacked low outside. He retreated with not quite panic, but something in that realm, on his face. His flustered state was his demise, for her quick advance had him retreating again. Attack. Parry. Riposte. And then an advance-lunge caused him to retreat again, but he tripped on his own foot, and with a yelp he fell to the ground in a heap. She saw how his ankle had turned when he fell, and it didn't look good.

The bout was over. Perhaps more than that. No man wanted to be bested—nay, humiliated—in such a fashion by a woman. No man's pride could take such a beating.

But she couldn't ease up on him. She wasn't the type to let someone else win when she was clearly the better athlete. At least in this sport. If he wanted to win, he would have to earn it. If he wanted to court her, he had to earn that, too. And hadn't she conceded her sisters' point that if she wanted to know him, she needed to reveal herself to him as well? What a terrible concession. Look what it had led to. A grown man on his arse at her hand. It was almost amusing except that it was vexing beyond belief.

He was the catalyst of some very aggravating changes in herself of late. She just wanted to know the truth. What was he about? But she was too irritated to push him today. She had probably pushed him to his limits already anyway.

"That's three," she stated. Not triumphantly. Not pitifully. Just as a fact. She put out her hand to help him up, knowing his ankle would be sore.

With a grunt, he pushed himself to standing and gingerly took a step. He winced. And then he cursed.

"Are you all right?"

"I'm fine."

He was fine. She was fine.

Everyone was fine.

WESLEY DID HIS utmost to disguise the limp in his gait as he left

Boudicca's house. That had been such a disaster. His pride had never been struck from so many angles, with such rapidity. He was not the kind to lay down in defeat, yet he had literally lain at her feet. Defeated. Again.

It was all the more reason to continue fencing. He would most certainly learn something from her and her style of combat. Hopefully, it would give him enough of an edge to claim victory over Samuel in the upcoming tournament. Speaking of Samuel, the four of them had an engagement planned this afternoon.

Really, the last thing he wanted to do was meet his Betting Buddies for lunch now. But he did need to eat. And he was not one to renege on his commitments.

And they were not the kind to let things slide.

"What's the limp all about?" James asked before Wesley could even sit down.

"Mind if I get a drink first, James?" He ordered a brandy and sat back in his seat, still under their scrutiny.

"Did you fall?" Chris asked.

"Yes."

Samuel must have caught something in his tone or in his face because he followed up with his own interrogation. "How did you fall?"

"I was fencing."

"Ah...practicing for the upcoming tournament were you? Do you think you can beat me this time?" Samuel was already digging for a bet. "Shall we place a wager on it?" He made a point to peer down at Wesley's foot. "Or will your injury heal in time?"

"I'm fine." Wesley straightened his spine. "I'll be ready, and I'll win. So you had better prepare to pay up if you're planning to put a wager on it."

Samuel laughed. "Right." He looked around the table. "So, anyone in for one hundred pounds?"

James and Chris both bet on Samuel, the traitors.

"Where were you fencing?" Chris asked and then took a bite of his mint and fennel mackerel.

His friends were many things, but gossips they were not. So Wesley deemed it safe to divulge Boudicca's secret.

"Where do you think? Who have I been with every morning since the bet we made?"

"Boudicca?" James' eyebrows shot upward while Chris continued eating.

"Come to think of it…" Wesley turned to Chris. "You probably already knew this secret, didn't you? With how familiar you are with the family."

Chris neither confirmed nor denied the accusation.

"Are there any other secrets I need to know about?"

"Nothing that I know of."

"Couldn't be more helpful than that, I suppose?"

Chris smiled and shook his head.

"I appreciate that you're a man of few words, but I could use a couple if you have any to spare."

"Well, all I can say about Boudicca is that she's always on guard."

"Yes, I've noticed."

"You know, she's actually a lot like you." Chris hugged one arm across his body. "You're both competitive."

"Yes, I've noticed that as well."

Chris threw up his hands. "Well, what else do you want to know if you know it all?"

How to win her over. How to get a kiss out of her. How to beat her in a bout.

"Never mind." He stuffed a piece of mackerel into his mouth. "I don't know why I bothered asking."

"Really, Wes. I don't recall the last time I saw you this irritated." James stared at him.

"Haven't been sleeping the greatest." He rubbed his back where his recent sleep on the settee had caused a small kink in his shoulder.

"You're not usually easily rattled. There's not a chance that the chit is getting under your skin, is there?"

"No. Not a chance."

"Don't say you're backing out of the bet? She's quite the kraken, but she can't be too much for you to manage, can she?"

"I can manage."

"He's probably just upset that she beat him in the fencing match," Samuel jested, not knowing his conjecture was actually the truth. When the three laughed and Wesley didn't join in, Samuel's laughter turned to shock.

"She didn't," he whispered reverently, "did she?"

Wesley couldn't bring himself to admit his defeat. It was one thing to lose in front of her, and she could gloat about it in her own mind, and likely to her sisters. It was another entirely for that victory to be more publicly advertised.

"Right, Samuel. Like I'd lose to a chit."

"I wouldn't put it past her," Chris said. "She's a master wielding a blade."

"So you do know more? Is it just a selective sharing then?" Wesley asked, aggravated.

James slapped Wesley on the shoulder, "Settle yourself, Wes." He chuckled. "The chit has you riled up and she's not even here. I would say she's got her claws in you, though I don't know how she did it."

"There are no claws, and there's nothing under my skin. It's just this cursed ankle, that's all. It needs to be elevated." As much as it pained him to admit a weakness of any kind, it was better to blame his foul mood on his physical pain than the real source of his irritation. "It'll be all right tomorrow."

"As long as you don't fall apart on me old man, I can't wait to take you on in the tournament. It's always a good day when I win. Though I must say, it won't be quite as satisfying if you're injured. Oh, I'll still take the win, don't misunderstand me, but it just won't quite have that same"—he punched a hand into his palm—"oomph. You know what I mean?"

Wesley knew exactly what he meant. The two were cut from the same cloth. Obnoxious competitors. So Samuel's taunting only fueled a demand inside of himself to be better. Do more. Mostly, the dynamic was healthy. It was a good thing Wesley came for lunch. He had a growing fire lit under his arse to win both the tournament and the bet.

His ankle would be better tomorrow. He would will it better, and he would fence with Boudicca. And then he would win. Whatever it was that needed to be won, he would win it. That's all that mattered.

CHAPTER ELEVEN

THE NEXT MORNING, Boudicca was so restless, it required an immediate jaunt over to the Practice Hall where she started in on squats. Fifteen repetitions. No, twenty. Her regular routine was usually a light warm up, a precursor to the activity of a practice match. This morning she needed to push herself to feel drained before it even began the fight because her body felt like a pianoforte upon which someone was clunking away and the reverberations were unceasing. She felt a mottled mess. Not knowing whether the duke was calling on her today was especially irksome. If she pushed herself hard enough in some rigorous exercise, perhaps her body would realign itself and she would feel normal.

She wasn't even sure what normal was. Proper ladies didn't fence to begin with. They didn't wear breeches. They didn't do all the things Boudicca loved to do. She knew there were other women like herself, her sister for example, but she hadn't discovered them yet because proper ladies didn't even speak about what proper ladies didn't do. Unless they were gossiping. Which coincidentally, proper ladies often did.

She should have gone out and paid calls. That was normal. She shuddered. There was a reason she didn't do that. It was more painful to sit and listen to idle gossip than to pretend she wasn't sitting at home waiting for Wesley. Besides, the *on dit* was likely to be about her, so what benefit did it serve to either her or the tattlemongers if the object of their gossip was present? So she stayed home and her sisters went out for the morning.

A knock on the door interrupted her twentieth count. Mid-squat, Wesley entered the gymnasium.

She popped up, feeling awkward about her bottom being pointed directly at him. "I didn't think you were coming today." She made a point to peer down at his ankle.

He lifted it up as if for inspection. "It's fine." And then he twisted it around to prove his mobility. "I've been here the last several mornings. My intentions are clear. Why wouldn't I come today?"

"There is that explicit comment about intentions again. How do I know what your intentions are?"

"I've told you."

"You could be lying."

"I'm not."

"You could be hiding something."

With a small huff, he walked over to her. "I told you that I'm courting you. What more do you need?"

"I need to know why." There. She had said it. It was about time, too. She berated herself for not asking this sooner. So many women would have loved to have his attention. They fought for it. In ways the *ton* did. A dropped fan here, an eye fluttering there. She had witnessed it, though never participated. It was imperative to uncover his secret.

What's not to court?"

His cavalier response sounded oddly, and terrifyingly similar to, what's not to love? But she shook that nonsensical sentiment out of her head. Thankfully he continued on.

"You're a well-figured woman with a sharp mind. You come from a wealthy and noble family. And…no one can accuse you of being boring."

It was a swarm of half-compliments. He had stated, more or less, indisputable facts. But it wasn't enough.

"Why do *you* want to court me?"

"I'm quite certain I just explained that."

"If those were reasons enough to court me, then every eligible bachelor would be here or would have attempted a courtship. What I want to know is, why do those particular traits in *me* compel *you* to be here? There must be a reason."

And she swore she saw him retreat to the tiniest degree. That tiniest degree ensconced him in a wordless bubble of the gymnasium. A vacuum, devoid of a lexicon. Just as it was discovered a half century ago that a person could not breathe in space, so Wesley could not form words in his current environment. This did not bode well for him. If a person could not answer a question in their normal tone and demeanor, they were hiding something. Boudicca knew. She was an expert in detecting ulterior motives.

She held out her hand and began counting her appendages. One. "You're not in need of my dowry."

He scoffed.

Two. "You're not clamoring for status."

Three. "You're not looking for a quick…fix." She prided herself on not blushing over that one.

Four. "No one has forced you into this."

Five. "Botheration! Why the deuce are you here?"

He was rigid. No tells. Not even one.

"Today, I'm here to fence. Shall we drown in a conversation where you're digging for something that doesn't exist? Or can you accept my intentions as they are so we can fence?" He was towering over her, not intentionally intimidating, but large, brawny, and exacting all the same. She would not take a step back from his muscular body that was radiating an immense amount of heat.

She knew he was hiding something. She could feel it in her bones. If he had lies and secrets, so too could she.

"Well, court all you want. But don't propose unless you're keen on rejection."

"What's this?"

"I'll not marry you."

"Why?"

Throwing part of his line back at him, she said, "I'm here to fence. Not sit around and talk."

He was a decent match and she wanted the practice. That part wasn't a lie. If he could forge ahead with their farce of a courtship, then surely she could do the same.

They strode to the piste and faced off. There was a new ill in the air today. Not a thrill. Not a chill, but a trill. A vibration. A thrumming that resounded through her.

Their bouts were by no means equal; she won every time, but he was attentive. Fastidious, even, to observing her every movement. Mimicking her. Losing. Failing. Yet trying again. And the losing didn't register in her mind; rather, she admired his determination. He was a true competitor.

At the end of it, they were both perspiring, and therefore rehydrating themselves.

"It's impressive that you showed up again today."

"I told you I was court—"

"Not to court me. To fence. You must know I'm the better fencer, and that I was bound to win. Again."

"True. I can't deny it, though it pains me to admit it."

"Yet you'll work at this, even though you're not good at it."

"I take exception to that statement. I'd say I'm a rather good fencer. But you are better." They stood nearly toe to toe at the water station. "You can't tell me that you have never done something you know you're not good at. When learning a new skill, everyone has to start from somewhere, and usually it's the bottom. Wouldn't you prefer to excel in a new skill than remain weak in it?"

Yes. Kissing.

Oh, that wretched thought should be blasted from her mind. But she couldn't help it. The thought had lunged into her mind and attacked high inside. It was a skill she didn't have, and perhaps it was a skill she could have...

Ack. She blotted the thought from her mind.

"Go change. We're done for today."

He turned to go behind the screen, and she strode off to quit the room. Only after reaching for the handle did she realize she hadn't put her sword away. She jaunted over to the watering station. When she heard male voices from outside the gymnasium, she panicked. It sounded like her father. She had thought he'd been away for the morning. Of course, he knew about her fencing, but she didn't think he would be too keen to know that the Duke of Baskim had been partnering with her.

What a thought? As if Wesley had been a partner of any kind. But that thought was quite low on the list of urgent items. Right now, she didn't want to face her father with the duke, so she snuck behind the screen bumping into Wesley in the small space.

And not a second too late.

Her father entered the gymnasium. He must have scanned the room, and seeing no one closed the door, for she heard him muttering, "I swear I heard someone in there." But to whomever he was muttering, he just continued listening and the voices faded down the corridor.

And then she realized...

Her hands were on skin. Perspiration coated skin. Warm, wet skin. One hand was on a stomach that felt as hard as granite. Yet there was soft curling hair down there. Down there. God, and it was leading further down. She could see the hairs curling over his breeches and leading down...down...down. She looked up to catalog where her other hand rested. Sigh. A thick, flexing bicep. She rubbed her thumb, advancing and retreating down a one inch path. It was real. She could feel it. Moving.

And then she looked up...

Into his eyes. Those piercing eyes. His pupils were dilated in shock. His nostrils flared.

"What are you doing?"

"I—I heard someone coming."

"I thought that your family expected this kind of behavior

from you."

"Expected. Yes. Observed me with a man. No." Her answers were short, not for lack of trying to explain, but for lack of oxygen to her brain. His scent, soap and hard work were overtaking her senses. So much so that she hadn't even removed her hands from his body. "I—I mostly fence with my tutor. My father would have been more than a little astonished to see you here. With me. Like this."

Like this. With her hands on his statuesque figure. Yet she still couldn't bring herself to retreat.

"Like this." His gaze dropped to her lips. "Or like this?"

And then his hands were on her. One resting firmly on the small of her back, his fingers dangerously close to her bottom. The other clasped around the back of her neck. And he swung her around and pushed her gently up against the wall, still encased behind the screen.

She gasped.

He leaned in closer to her lips. He was offering a second chance. It was an invitation though, not a demand, for he left space between them. Hardly any. But there was space. And although the space was less than an inch apart, it may as well have been a universe away. The space was the difference between a good girl and, well…a proper woman. Woman, not lady. All her life she had always been the good girl. Her only deviance from etiquette was her enjoyment of fencing. Soon, that deviation would be pronounced, and public, but she had time before that happened. And when it did, she would not again have a chance like the one presented before her. A kiss with a gentleman. Once her reputation was ruined, there was no going back.

So why not take the step from a good girl to a proper woman. As in, a woman with experience. Of the world. Of celestial proportions.

He was nice…enough. He was manliness personified. She knew of his rakish endeavors, which meant, if she were going to take the leap with someone, it may as well have the most potential as possible to be good. And really, he was here. Inviting her.

But the nail in the coffin was her final thought. The courtship was all a sham anyway. Why not milk it for all it was worth?

And then, feeling as if she were the first woman to travel in space, she took the interstellar step.

CHAPTER TWELVE

EITHER WESLEY GREW impatient and moved in at the same time, or Boudicca overestimated the space between them. That or she was just destined to be bad at this whole kissing thing. She would never know the real reason for her first kiss being an unfortunate bumbling mess. But she was pretty sure that her chin chucked his lips and her nose gouged his eye. All the while his hands remained locked in place. A soft rumble reverberated from his chest, which, now that she thought about it, was lodged nicely against her bosoms. And now that she really thought about it, her nipples had tipped into peaks. And yes, that slight bit of friction against his chest was about to lead to her demise.

"Boudicca,"—he leaned his forehead against hers—"this is not a bout. There's no attacking here." His lips were practically grazing hers, they were so close. "May I?"

She nodded slowly, causing his head to follow her movements.

And then she had her real first kiss. Not a bump or a bunglement of orifices.

His lips gently swept hers at the corner of her mouth. "So soft," he said. And her body responded by wilting.

She slid her hands to meet together at his chest. Her fingers ran through his chest hairs like velvet. And just like with the teasing fabric, she couldn't leave it alone.

His lips were pressing against hers, parting. And he moaned, while bringing his body closer to hers. His hips. Closer to her center, covered only in one light layer of clothing.

"I'm very thankful for these trousers you're wearing," he growled into her ear.

And she could feel his thankfulness. And he felt very thankful. In fact, his significant thankfulness was grinding up against her cleft, and she felt herself growing quite…appreciative.

His lips, once soft and gentle, were growing more ravenous. They parted more and she gasped at his scent of mint. He pushed against her lips, letting himself into her mouth. His tongue swept in, teasing her. And she wanted him. She wanted to kiss the Adonis that he was, learning seduction from him the way he had been learning fencing from her. So she mimicked his movements until his groans saturated her.

Here she was, kissing the handsomest duke lauded by society. The woman, the spinster, who by all other gossip was on the shelf, not to be taken down again. Well, he had noticed her on the shelf for some inexplicable reason, and he had taken her down off of it to take a look at her. Who was she to deny herself the pleasure of being handled?

His hands gripped her thighs and pushed her up further against the wall. He stepped closer, in between her legs.

"Wrap your legs around me," he whispered.

And it was the most natural thing in the world to do so. To grip him between her thighs. To hang onto him, and to feel him, through the few layers, rubbing against her core. The layers were so thin, she could feel him, base to tip, as she pressed herself along his arousal.

His fingers pressed into her quads and squeezed. His moan didn't stop as his hands slid to massage her bottom. When one of his hands slid up to release her shirt from her trousers, the warm fingers against her skin shot through at a startling rate.

She tugged her lips free. "We have to stop." Her head fell lightly against the wall. Eyes closed. Breath hard.

He pressed a kiss to her chest. "Yes, we do."

She released her legs from his hips, and he stood back. He pulled on his shirt and ran his fingers through his hair.

He opened his mouth to say something.

"Don't."

"You don't know what—"

"It doesn't matter. Don't say anything. Don't claim honor and ask me to marry you. And don't say you weren't going to do that. Even if you weren't. I don't want to know."

And she really didn't want to know. If he were an honorable gentleman, he would have asked her to marry him. Honor demanded it. But no one had witnessed their actions, so he could get away without asking her. But did she want to know that he was that kind of man? No. Right now she wanted to know if he was the kind of man to respect her wishes. Demands, really. And he owed her that much. And now she saw her opportunity to exploit the situation. If it was a sham—which it was—then it would be a damn good sham for her.

Her sisters had been wrong. She had shown herself to him, and he was still holding back. So be it. She could put her guards up again. It was easy. She literally trained nearly every day in putting her guards up. This would be no different. But if he was getting something out of this, besides the fencing lessons he hadn't explicitly asked for, then—botheration!—she would get something out of this too. Damn it. And since she now knew what she could get, all that remained was to ask for it.

Ask and ye shall receive.

"All right…"

"This is what we're going to do." She placed her hands on her hips. "You want to continue these fencing lessons—"

"I wouldn't call them lessons—"

Really, the man could be a bit obtuse. "What would you call it when a person meets privately with someone to study and mimic their expertise in a specific field with the objective of improving their own skills?"

"Observ—"

"Don't." She held up her hand. "Please, don't insult my intelligence. We'll continue your...lessons." She narrowed her eyes at him. "And because you owe me—"

"I owe you? For what?"

"For the lessons."

He crossed his arms, clearly not having bought into the lessons business.

"And because you owe me"—she rushed to say—"for the lessons, you can give me some lessons of my own."

"In what?"

"Seduction."

AN ODD STRANGLED chortle-like sound tumbled out of his mouth. "Seduc—Wha—I think not." Folded arms should indicate his position on the matter. The kiss had been nice. His mind wouldn't wrap around a more apt word at the moment. So *nice*, it was. Passionate, in fact. And maybe that was the reason he didn't want it to happen again, but really...lessons in seduction? There was no way in hell that he was about to give the cursed gel some lessons in passion. It was an effrontery to his honor to even consider that. A person did not just engage in seduction lessons. It wasn't done.

"Not seduction exactly. Mostly just..." she waved her fingers around. "Kissing."

"I can't give you kissing lessons, Boudicca."

"And I can't give you fencing lessons, Wesley."

"You have been—"

"Exactly. And you just kissed me. Lessons will be the same as what we've both been doing."

They would likely not be the same as what they had just done because Wesley had never given kissing lessons before, and if he were to think about giving lessons they would not be given so urgently. With so much desire. He stamped that thought down.

"Lessons in passion—"

"Not passion. Just kissing."

"They're one and the same." Even he knew he was grasping at clouds, feeling lost in the argument.

"I don't think so."

"Since you're the kissing aficionado, do explain."

"Again. There's no need to insult me. I'm perfectly aware of my amateur status in kissing."

He wouldn't have said amateur exactly. She was a quick study. A natural, really.

"I'm sure you have had a kiss without passion, no?"

"True." He thought back to several experiences where there was no deeper connection than a kiss. More often than not, that kiss led nowhere and didn't happen again.

"In the same way, I'm sure you have had passion without a kiss, no?"

He genuinely had to stop and think about that one.

"Wesley, really? Are you saying that every time you have felt passionately toward someone you have kissed them?"

"I dare say that is true."

"You cannot be denied? Is that what you're claiming?"

"Well, I'm certainly not saying I ever forced myself on anyone." He glared at her. "I'll return your turn of phrase: don't insult me. I would never kiss a woman unless she also desired to kiss me."

He saw a slight flush run up her neck. Odd, that.

"Regardless," she said as she waved her finger in the air again, "passion and kissing are different. You can have one without the other. You agree."

"Yes."

"So teach me kissing without the passion."

"I can't do that." It wasn't a lie. It wasn't even a stall tactic.

"Figure out a way, Wesley, or the fencing lessons and this

ramshackle courtship are done."

"Fine." He wanted the lessons. He needed the lessons. He had to win. But which lessons and what precisely he had to win, he wasn't sure.

He would find a way to forge on, even knowing he couldn't shake the hunger that had erupted within him when he stole into her mouth and tasted her for the first time. He wanted to taste more of her. Perhaps all of her. But she was a gently bred young(ish) lady. He should have offered marriage, and really, that was the plan. That was the bet. He was here for the bet. But then he was here for the fencing. And apparently now he was here for the kissing.

He could feel his nostrils flaring. That was the only outward display of emotion he wanted to send her. And even that was too much. He couldn't let on that she was right in accusing him of ulterior motives.

He should have offered marriage, but what if she had said yes? He needed her to say no. If he could somehow turn her plan on her head, and scare her away, she might say no to the kissing lessons as well. With that taste in her mouth, he could propose knowing that she would say no. And then they would both go on their merry way. Him having won his bet, and her…well, it didn't matter, did it?

Something poked his chest. He looked down at her outstretched hand, an offer to shake on it.

"Do we have a deal?"

"No emotions. No conditions." He watched as she nodded along. "You teach—show me some fencing maneuvers, and I'll show you some…kissing."

"Precisely."

Feeling a decided lack of options, as well as a growing disdain for shaking hands on a deal, Wesley stuck out his hand, took hers, and shook. Hard. For extra measure.

"Fine. It's a deal."

And then almost as sweetly as he had first heard her voice on the night of the *bumping* ball, she said, "See you tomorrow then."

"Yes." See you. Fight you. Feel you. Kiss you. Just another normal day in a typical courtship.

CHAPTER THIRTEEN

HUMPHREY WELLS, EARL of Dalhone, more affectionately known as Father, had been mostly absent for the duke's visits. She had seen him over the last week, but it had been sparse. Sometimes he had a habit of hermitting himself in his study to read. Other times he busied himself with travel and historical research, usually about battles and weaponry.

Boudicca, along with the *ton*, knew he was a bit eccentric, and it sometimes caused gossip, but most of it wasn't too harmful. He trusted his daughters. Even more so now that Boudicca had been deemed a spinster and could act as her sisters' chaperone. But trust a parent to walk in on their daughter at the most humiliating moment. Up until the minute she was behind the screen, everything had been proper. Or at least close enough to it.

There hadn't been any wayward thoughts. At least not many. There hadn't been any lingering touches. At least not physical. And there certainly hadn't been any kisses. That didn't happen until later. And who should show up, throwing Boudicca into a panic over nothing, thus causing her most scandalous moment to date.

She should thank her father.

Not to his face of course. What would she say? *Thanks for walking in on me and causing me to act indecently with a man for the first time?* Or, *thanks for opening the door to my first kiss?* No, of course, she wouldn't say any of those things even though she was happy to have had her first kiss. But there must have been some little girl inside of her still looking for her father's approval, because that afternoon she sought him out.

She found him in his study, poring over history books.

"Who are you reading today?"

Grabbing a marker, he placed it in his book, and then looked up. "Boudicca, what a coincidence. I happen to be reading your namesake's biography."

"For the hundredth time?"

"Or thereabouts." A light smile trickled across his lips. "Were you just fencing?"

Startled, Boudicca was about to ask how he knew that, when she realized she was still in her gear. "Oh, yes. I was."

"I must have just missed you. Would have loved to watch you practice. It's been ages since I've seen you have a good match."

"Perhaps next time, Father."

"Yes. That would be nice." He dropped his head back to his book, more out of distraction than dismissal.

"Father," she started the sentence with no clue how she was actually going to phrase it. How would she ask for her father's permission to kiss a man? She didn't feel as though she needed his permission. It wasn't that. She just…well, it was all too new. And although she was usually decisive in most things, she faltered over this one.

"How did you know you wanted to marry Mama?"

He looked back up wistfully.

"Is it possible to have standards set too high?"

"Like the Duke of Baskim? I understand he's been around." He chuckled.

If Boudicca had any doubts about her father having his ear to the ground, they were answered. He may not know everything that was going on, but he also didn't know nothing about her current affairs.

"The duke, yes, that's likely less about standards and more

about connection. He's a man though. He won't admit to his feelings. He might say that he doesn't like a woman for…her hair, or some other silly thing. But what he means is that there was nothing about her that made him want to stick around. No connection. No feelings."

He chuckled again and tapped his fingers against the desk. "I'm only sharing feelings now in my old age."

"You're not old."

"I'm getting there. But that's beside the point. I must say, if it were only about standards, you would exceed his."

"You have to say that. You're my father."

"Perhaps." He covered his mouth as if to share a secret. "But I wouldn't have said the same thing about Artemisia." He winked.

"She meets a completely different set of standards." Boudicca smiled, thinking of her hellion of a sister. The pause was filled with her knee bouncing up and down as she thought. "What about my standards? Are they too high?"

"A woman should never settle. It's a man's duty to protect her and take care of her. You do yourself an injustice if you settle."

That wasn't what she wanted to hear. "What if my standards are preventing a man from getting to know me?" She smoothed her hands down her breeches, a useless tactic in subduing the shaking leg.

"The right man will know exactly how high to jump. And if he doesn't, he will continue to try. If he doesn't know or doesn't try, he's not the right man for you, Boudicca."

She should be grateful that there was no one forcing her to marry. That her father accepted her fate as a spinster or was encouraging her to find a true love match. She couldn't help but wonder what her mother would say. She might be pushing her right into the arms of Wesley, only to walk in on them and demand a ring. No, she wasn't really that kind. But Boudicca supposed any woman could act differently out of desperation, and she had known that her mother hoped to see her married.

"How much...erm—instruction should I give him? That is, about how high to jump?"

Her father chuckled. "I wish I could tell you what you need to hear, my dear. If only your mother were here..." he shook his head and let it fall into his hands.

"I would love for her to be here, but if she were, I'd still come to you and ask questions."

"I suppose that may be true. I shall leave you with this then. I knew I loved your mother from the moment she read the first book I ever gave her." He lifted the biographical tome in the air. "She had never heard of Boudicca before, yet she read the book." A warm smile filled his face. "Not only did she read it though, she said that Boudicca was a beautiful name and that she inspired her to reach for her destiny. And then she took my hand in hers. And I knew..." A soft sheen coated his eyes and a tear slipped out.

"She was the most wonderful woman I had ever met..." His voice was hoarse, and Boudicca could feel a lump forming in her throat.

"She was."

He stood and came out from behind his desk. Boudicca rose to meet him and his embrace. And then he said exactly what she needed to hear, "So, my dear, reach for your destiny. When you see it. And don't let go."

THE FENCING MATCH had gone well. Wesley felt as though he were improving his skills. If he gleaned even a few new moves, he could beat Samuel merely by taking points by surprise. And though he knew he had learned some new techniques today, he couldn't remember what they were. His foggy recollective abilities may have had something to do with an overwhelming sense of anticipation for their secondary lessons. He remembered some lunging and some ripostes. But what was really on his mind was plunging back into her mouth and posting her up against the wall.

Kissing lessons devoid of passion. That was what he was supposed to prepare for. And he had told himself that all evening and all morning. It was the night time that he had been unable to restrain.

He had not had dreams of something so innocent as flowers again. Though there had been rose petals strewn across the bed, now that he thought of it. And her. Boudicca had been lying in his bed in her breeches, through which he could make out the exact shape of her legs and the apex of her sex. He had woken up hard in the middle of the night. Aching, he took himself in hand. He told himself it was for the best, lest he bring all that passion to her and their kissing lesson.

"Water?"

The question drenched his dreams, rushing them away. He glanced up at her holding him a glass. He took it and gulped it down.

"Shall we...kiss?"

And her reply was all matter of fact. "Yes. Let's."

She reached for his hand and drew him behind the screen. When she leaned her back against the wall, he could see by the tilt of her head that she wasn't entirely sure of what she was doing.

"Do you still want to do this?"

"Yes. I've determined that it is the best way forward for my future to improve my skills in this area."

He leaned in and pressed his lips against hers as a hand flew to his chest.

"Wait."

He could sense that Boudicca was nervous. She wanted to kiss him. She wanted him to kiss her. He was one of the most powerful dukes of the *ton*, and he had a reputation with the ladies. Of course she would want attention—lessons—from the best of the best. "Is there no warm up?"

"This isn't fencing. There are no exercises to practice."

"Are you sure?"

"Quite sure."

"Well…um…if you had to start kissing me somewhere else, to um…warm up. Where could you start?"

This wasn't his plan. He didn't want to kiss her elsewhere. Lips were safe. Elsewhere led to passion.

"I thought you wanted kissing lessons without passion?"

"I do. But just um…show me my options."

Show me my options? The chit was driving him crazy. She wanted options? He would give her options. Passion be cursed!

And he intended to plant a few kisses harshly over her skin, and in using such a delivery none of them would appeal to her, so then he could kiss her right back on the lips where he had started. Safely.

The first kiss he placed roughly on her nose. Which, when he pulled back, caused an unexpected smile to form on her face. The smile tugged at his heart. No, not his heart. His insides somewhere. Anywhere other than his heart. So he placed another kiss on her ear. Notably less roughly. His breath must have tickled because her shoulders drew up and caught him by the jaw.

"Not there," she nearly giggled.

And he found himself wanting to kiss her exactly there again.

"I'll kiss you wherever I want to. I'm the one giving the lessons, aren't I? And you wanted your options." He kissed her against her ear again, much less roughly. One might even label it softly. Her giggle was also softer, but her shoulders pulled up again.

"These are in the way," he said as he pressed a kiss against her shoulder. "I need more access to this." And then he trailed excessively soft kisses up her neck where his lips could feel her smooth exposed skin.

Her sigh impelled him to step closer, so he could feel her breasts push up against his chest. His hands gripped her waist, holding her still. Forcing her not to move into him more than he could control.

So not to leave one side unattended, he kissed the other side of her neck, trailing kisses until he reached her collar.

"Are there other options?" she asked in a gravelly voice.

"Plenty." He tripped a finger down the buttons of her shirt. "May I?"

Her eyes widened but her head nodded.

With each button he loosened, he kissed a new inch of exposed skin. By the time his lips were on the top of her breasts, her hands were in his hair.

"Wesley," she gasped. And he hadn't even gotten to the good part yet. With his name on her lips, he was lost to any plans he had crafted. Plans, what plans? The only thing on his mind was seeing how many times he could get her to say his name.

One of his hands reached up to bring her breast to his mouth. His tongue flicked her nipple.

"Wesley!"

He licked again.

"Wesley!"

Waiting for his grin to fade, he pulled her nipple into his mouth and sucked. And then she groaned into his ear, and he had a new goal.

Chapter Fourteen

THE HOTTEST DUKE she had ever seen had his mouth suckling her nipple. Her body felt faint at the thought, but her mind would not succumb to darkness because it wanted to be alert for every lick. Every nibble. Every—

"Ah, Wesley. Oh my God." He sucked on her other breast, while his hand kneaded the first one. As if his mantra were *no throb goes unattended*.

In that case, maybe she needed to keep giving him an indication that there was an ache, much lower, and much throbbier, that needed consideration. But could she be so wicked as to ask for attention to be paid to that part of her? A part of her that she herself hardly ever touched. And certainly no one else had noticed. How could she be so wicked—

A groan thrummed through her. He didn't need any instructions apparently. His fingers danced across her mons, presumably looking for the buttons to her falls. Once found, he tucked his fingers under the fabric and slid a finger down in between her curls.

One hand on her breast. One hand playing with her core. And his mouth, searing into hers. He had said kissing was not an attack, but this felt like a full onslaught of sensations, in the best possible way. If it was a battle, it was one she was absolutely willing to yield to. Let the man do as he pleased, for everything he touched ebbed and flowed with ache and stimulation.

He was devouring her with his mouth. Something about her, about her body at least, appealed to him. He was like a starving man being presented a feast. His finger was sliding between her folds, down and up. When he rubbed back up her, ooh so deliciously slowly, his thumb tapped gently on her nub. And then circled around it. And then circled it, and oh, her body was laid siege. He groaned into her mouth and pressed her harder against the wall. She could feel his throbbing member against her thigh.

With no understanding of how to alleviate the ache she suspected he had, she yanked on his shirt and clawed her hands down his chest, which dislodged his mouth from hers.

Thankfully, it was for only as long as it took for him to grumble, "You are a goddess."

She ran her hands down his chest. Through his soft curls. Needing him. Wanting more touch. More exposure. Real closeness. His body was perfect. A thought she had never considered about a man that she knew. A Corinthian body. Only taller than her by a few inches, but stronger by half. In his arms, she felt small, but fierce. Womanly. He had tapped into her body, and somehow that was transferring to her mind and heart.

A goddess he had said.

And she felt like one. Only in his arms. Powerful. Coveted.

He was the man with the highest standards of anyone in the *ton*, yet he was here. There was nowhere else she wanted to be. Ulterior motives forgotten. Dares forgotten. Fencing forgotten. Kissing lessons forgotten. Everything but his touch. Forgotten.

Maybe there was a chance he liked her. It was the most ridiculous thought. Regardless, it nestled itself in her head. No, it burrowed itself in her head like an ant set on finding and building a home for its queen.

His mouth trickled down her neck for a soft bite. But she longed for his mouth and moaned his departure.

"I'm here," he mumbled, returning to her lips.

Every possible way to find closeness to him. She opened for him. Hot. Wet. And down in her core, she felt herself change.

Soften. As her body responded to his touch, she felt the pinnacle was just out of reach.

"Wesley," she murmured against his lips. "Wesley." It was a plea. "Wesleeeey."

And he knew how to answer her pleas.

She yanked her lips from him and shouted. Absolute release. A complete and total loss of control. It was nothing she had known before. Her body shuddered. She had given a part of herself to him that she could never get back.

He had defeated her, and she had never known defeat could feel so sweet.

THEY WERE SUPPOSED to attend a garden party that afternoon, Boudicca and her sisters. The Countess of Linsgate always threw a splendid garden party. Slightly knobby chairs, but the food was always delicious, and the guests always handpicked.

After the kissing lesson however—which really, how could she call it a lesson anymore?—she wasn't too keen on a garden party. She felt a starry eyed dreamer, wanting to sit in her room and relive the kiss over and over again.

But she wouldn't.

It *had* been a lesson. He hadn't indicated otherwise. So she needed to treat it as such and move forward with her life Perhaps one lesson would suffice. Lord knew it would suffice for providing memories for quite a while. If that's all it amounted to, that was acceptable. Maybe more so than acceptable.

"Boudicca," Artemisia shouted from the bottom of the stairs. "Are you ready yet? The carriage is ready."

Ladies do not shout, Boudicca wanted to cant back. Instead, she took an extra moment to reaffix a bow in her hair, and then she strode down the stairs. She was in for an afternoon of tedious gossip, which would require fastidious vigilance of her daydreaming.

Joan glanced up, "Boudicca, you look lovely." There was some astonishment in her voice.

"It's just an old dress." She was an idiot for saying that. Her sisters knew her wardrobe, and she was not wearing just an old dress. She was wearing one of her best dresses for a garden party. Not an evening gown, but something with a little more scandal than she might otherwise have worn had she not been kissed senseless so recently.

Boudicca hoped that the ride to the garden party did not portend the afternoon's events, for she was being bombarded with questions. Some subtle, while others not so much.

"Was the duke here this morning?" Subtle. From Joan.

"Yes. We had a nice match. I think he's improving his skills."

"Is that his goal?" Zenobia asked, innocently, yet coyly.

"He's very competitive. His goal is always to improve."

"Sounds like you." Zenobia said. "He's known to have incredibly high standards. You're quite special to have garnered more than one visit. Let alone four."

"Seven." That correction had been a mistake.

"You've been counting?" Mimi was on the edge of her seat. "So you like him then? I mean, who doesn't? But still...*you* like him. Imagine, the two people among the *ton* with the highest standards falling for each other. It makes sense I suppose."

"I'm not falling for him."

"Right." Not so subtle. "Have you kissed him?" Mimi stared directly at her.

There was no hiding it. Oh, she tried to hide it. Good Heavens, how she wished she could have hid it. Soon it would be known that she, the eldest, the spinster, the good girl, the one keeping them all in line, the prim and proper one was...a wanton.

"Oh my God, Bodi! You did kiss him. I can't believe it." Mimi's limbs were swinging. Nobi retreated to the squabs to avoid a finger in the eye.

And Boudicca thought Mimi was going to add, *How could you?*

I can't believe it. You're such a canting hypocrite.

Instead, she added, "I can't believe how happy I am for you." Was that a tear she saw in Mimi's eyes?

"It's not that big of a deal." Wait. That was also the wrong thing to say. Kissing was a big deal.

"It's a bit of a deal," Joan said with a smile. "Did you like it?"

"How could I not?" The words slipped out, causing the sisters to chuckle. She was so lucky to have such a tight-knit family with sisters like friends. Often she felt too greatly the responsibility of being the eldest. Leading the way. Modeling the best behavior. It was a relief to let go and just be. Just feel. Just do.

It was not the way of the *ton*. But it should be the way of their family.

"So it's a real thing, then?" Nobi asked.

She shrugged. "Honestly, I have no idea what's real anymore. But my feelings, I guess, are real."

Mimi was crying. Boudicca saw her swipe at her eyes.

"What are the tears for?"

"I'm just so happy for you. You deserve to be happy. I hope it's true love."

"Thank you." While she didn't think it was true love, maybe it was, just a little more than like. "Now dry those eyes, we have a garden party to attend."

The sisters alit the carriage, Mimi discreetly fanning her eyes (as inconspicuous as that motion can be). Immediately, they were greeted by their hostess, and the Countess of Linsgate was exceptionally loquacious today.

"It's a delight to have you four here. I believe I have the perfect guestlist today." Her hands were a flutter, almost a clap, but no sound.

"My daughter, Lady Simone, as I'm sure you know, has her pick of *all* the eligible bachelors. And then some."

Lady Simone was quite lovely. Almost the opposite of Boudicca. Petite brunette to Boudicca's tall blonde.

Unsure of how to respond to the countess' claim of *and then some*, Boudicca merely nodded her head.

After greeting their hostess and finding a table, the sisters sat amiably and chatted with a few friends.

"Remember not to stare at him, Zenobia. Christopher will make his way over here eventually. He's a friend." Boudicca half-admonished, half-encouraged her sister.

"I wonder who he's with...all I can see are the backs of their heads." Mimi was straining her neck and altogether staring at Christopher, albeit not all doe-eyed like Nobi.

"They're all dukes. The Betting Buddies I hear them called," Joan said.

"You do? Where do you hear them called that?" Mimi curiously turned her attention to Joan.

But Joan merely shrugged. "Around. If you were a bit older..." she let the teasing phrase hang in the air.

"I've been around nearly as long as you have."

"Sisters," Boudicca hissed, "please keep it to yourself. I've never heard of them, and I've been around the longest. Joan's probably pulling your leg. If you let go, she'll fall on her bottom." She threw Joan a smile, and the sisters continued their bickering in a hush.

Boudicca brought her teacup to her lips, and trembled at the thought of her kiss earlier. It wasn't as easy as she had hoped to not think about him. His thick rippling muscles and his sandalwood scent. With an inhale, she could practically smell him. Perhaps another guest in attendance wore a similar fragrance to him.

Him.

There he stood. Right in front of her. He dipped his head and gave a half smile.

Mimi was giddy beside her. "Did you see that?" she hissed at Boudicca as if her heart wasn't already in her throat.

Wesley tipped his head to one of the refreshment tables with raised brows. Oh my God, he wanted to speak to her again. Now. They had just seen each other a couple of hours ago. His gesture had communicated a question, so she nodded.

She tried not to watch as he approached the refreshment table, filled a plate, and sauntered over to them.

Ever the gentleman, he greeted those at the table and then set before her a plate of pistachio ice.

Her favorite. He remembered? She had mentioned it, but it had been so brief.

Her eyes sought his, unable to hide the question.

"It's your favorite, right?" he whispered.

He eased himself into the chair beside her. And from the half-lidded look he was giving her, she thought for sure he was going to feed her a spoonful.

Thank God for Mimi. "How lovely! I didn't realize they had ices."

"Just served," he said.

"And pistachio. That's Bodi's favorite."

"Really? I had no idea." He turned to his own flavor, white coffee, and took a bite.

Mimi poked her in the ribs and whispered, "I think I know something real when I see it."

"He's just here as a guest. He's here for the"—she strained to think of what he could possibly be here for when saying *tea party* didn't quite fit—"fun." That was bathetic.

"Right. And I'm here for the comfortable chairs." Mimi scoffed. "He's here for you, Bodi. Just accept it."

Well, he wasn't here for fencing. And likely not kissing. So...perhaps, just maybe, he was here for her. She smiled.

"That good?" Wesley leaned closer, brushing her arm as he moved.

"Delicious. Thank you."

"You mentioned you were coming today."

Her heart pounded. He was here just for her. That notion was surreal. A dream. A fantasy. Something she had given up long ago. Or maybe, had never even truly allowed herself to have. Adonis had his eyes set on her. Her head was swimming.

She took a quick look around and noticed several discrete pairs of eyes on her. The Countess of Linsgate. Lady Simone. And a few more envious looks. She had never been the center of such attention and envy. People vying to catch a glimpse of something that would later turn into gossip.

She had to maintain a prim and proper disposition. It had never been more difficult. It had never been easier than with him.

"Do you really like the white coffee, Your Grace?"

His eyes didn't budge from hers. "It's delicious. I think I want more."

CHAPTER FIFTEEN

Boudicca sat in front of the mirror pulling a few brushstrokes through her hair. It had been quite the irregular afternoon. Up until the garden party, most of their time had been spent alone, or at least, privately. But there, sipping tea together, and him bringing her a treat had felt…different. And he had brought her a taste of her favorite flavored ice. For everyone to see. And many were observing and speculating. Surely there would be gossip spilling out of this afternoon's event.

The most peculiar aspect of the ice escapade was that it was one of the least scandalous things they had done together, yet it would be the topic of gossip. More scandalous actions included the following: she had worn breeches in front of him, they had fenced, she had won, and of course, they had kissed. That was patently the most scandalous of all so far.

All her life, her public life, Boudicca had followed the rules. Prim. Proper. Responsible. But some rules were just meant to be broken. The rules she broke were only ever for herself, namely the breeches and the fencing. One day she would work up enough nerve to go public with those actions, but she needed a bit more time. It was a dream to instill confidence in other women. Empower young girls. Girls were always praised for being beautiful, as if that were the highest possible achievement. Boudicca had always felt within her a need to be a force. It was the very essence within her that people perceived as intense. The essence she subdued, all but when she was fencing. Hence her plans for an academy.

Enjoying her ruminations in solitude too much, Boudicca was surprised when without warning, there was a short knock on the door, no time to reply, and then Mimi. In the middle of her room.

"What are you doing here? It's late," Boudicca said.

Without a word, Mimi rushed over to the window and flicked something that sounded almost like the click of a lock.

"Mimi, what are you doing?"

And sure enough…"I'm unlocking your window."

"Why?"

"Why?" Mimi's eyes popped out of their sockets. "How can you even ask that? What if the duke decides to show up in your room tonight only to find your window locked? You might be asleep and not hear him. What will he think then? He may think you're turning down his advances."

Boudicca's leg started bouncing at the same rate as her heart was pounding. "He would never…"—she shook her head—"no, he wouldn't…"

"He might…"

"No."

"He could."

"He wouldn't."

"Bodi, I saw the way he was looking at you today. You have spent time together every day. You've," she darted a glance around the clearly empty room, "kissed." The last word was unnecessarily whispered.

Boudicca rolled her eyes. She should have never told her sisters about the kiss. Especially Mimi. She would only contrive some hopeless fantasy over it all.

"If he came—if'—she held up her hand—"if, it's a hypothetical Bodi, what would you do?"

"I would turn down his advances if he came through my window at night."

"Any night? Or just tonight?" She hadn't even flinched at

Bodi's reply, already having a secondary question prepared.

Exasperated, Boudicca released a ragged sigh. "Out with you."

"I just want to make sure you're ready if he does come." She swiftly looked down at Boudicca's nightrail. "You're not wearing that, are you?"

"It's night time. I'm going to sleep. This," Boudicca pulled on the sides of her most comfortable cotton nightrail, "is what I'm wearing. To sleep."

"But—"

And then realizing the only logical way to get Artemisia out of the room was to apply Mimi's own argument against her, Boudicca said, "If he does come, the last person he will want to find in my room is you."

"But—" Artemisia held up her index finger as if she had a tertiary argument. Silence. "No, that's a perfectly good point."

Having pushed her sister across the room and toward the door, they were nearly there...yes, the doorframe was within reach. Boudicca used it as leverage.

"Just don't lock the window," Mimi commanded.

"All right," Boudicca sighed.

"And change. Please. For the love of God, change."

"All right!" Boudicca whispered sharply.

She closed the door and leaned against it, resting her head against the wood.

What an imagination that girl had. The duke would never visit her chambers in the middle of the night. That would be the most asinine behavior she could ever conceive of him. He was a duke. A powerful, sought-after-by-all duke. They had shared one kiss. He wasn't going to come to her room tonight. Or any night.

Boudicca looked down at her nightrail and used her hands to smooth the lines of the worn fabric down her thighs. Searching for and finding one loose thread in the nightrail, she changed out of it.

It was the most moronic, imbecilic, foolhardy, some might even say, asinine, thing he had ever done.

His gentle tap on the window was the loudest sound in the dark of night.

He didn't hear anything, so he tried the window. It was eeking open. It was unlocked? But the thought didn't have time to register because as he was pushing the window open, so was she.

"Wesley?" Bewilderment encrusted her query.

"Yes. It's me." He hopped into her room. The first thing he noticed was her nightrail. It wasn't a tattered old cotton article that he had been expecting. The one she wore looked almost new. There were no sleeves. He sucked in a breath. And it had a few bows on it. Ties. That he could pull to unwrap her. And, by God, he was pretty sure he could see the outline of her impressive breasts in it. He couldn't help staring, and as he did, his imagination of them turning turgid became a reality. And he could feel his cock swelling.

"What are you doing here?" she crossed her arms over her glorious nipples.

He cleared his throat. "I came to...talk."

"You came to my room in the middle of the night to talk?"

"Yes."

"Really. Won't we talk tomorrow?"

"Yes. But we have our lessons. And then there's a ball tomorrow evening..." he was rambling like the biggest idiot he had ever seen. What had become of him? The man with the highest standards. The duke who had never courted a lady.

"I dare say you have ulterior motives."

"I might."

"Just be honest then."

"I couldn't wait until tomorrow to kiss you again." There. He had said it. It sounded stupider out of his mouth than inside his head. What was twelve hours to wait?

"All right. You want us to have another kissing lesson then? I suppose you do owe me a few, so catching up is a good idea."

"Let's be clear about one thing. This is not a lesson."

"It's not." Half-question.

"No. I—um…was unable to separate passion and the lesson. This—me coming to you at night—is me coming as a man interested in a woman."

He couldn't very well have said gentleman and lady, for in no way were his intentions that honorable. And if they did become intimate and he proposed, doing the honorable thing, he knew she would decline the offer. She had already told him as much. It seemed a win-win, if she wanted it as much as he did.

"You're not a gentleman tonight?"

"No," he said, stepping closer to her. "But if you're a lady, I'll do the honorable thing and leave you in peace." He slipped a finger under the strap of her nightrail. If one could even call it that. He didn't ask how she acquired it. He was just thankful she had it. He pressed a kiss to her neck, remembering that she liked that option.

Her hands slowly came up to his neck, and her eyes closed as she tilted her head to grant him better access. "I don't think I'm a lady tonight. You make me feel too much a woman."

He growled in response and bit her neck softly. His cock was already aching, wanting to press against her, slide through her, and into her if she wanted it.

"You lead. I already know what I would have us do tonight. But I know this is new for you."

"I don't know what there is to do. As much as it chagrins me to admit it, it's better if you lead. I'll follow."

"The mighty Boudicca," he whispered into her ear, "will follow my lead?" He was teasing her, of course. But there were layers of truth laced into his jest. He was a man with incredibly high standards. He commanded people to act and they did. He could have any woman he wanted, if he wanted any woman. Yet here he was, stupefied, falling for the most challenging woman he had ever met.

She had her own standards. And though they clashed against his, they didn't undermine him. Not only that, she had her own set of rules by which she lived her life. Ever the perfect face in public, she broke rules when it was important to her. The woman was a master fencer and no one knew. God, she was brilliant.

And he was…

"I'm humbled, Boudicca. That you would follow me."

"I trust you. In this."

The words that had the potential to soar him to the highest heights stung. She trusted him. In this. Yet it was all accurate. She should only trust him in this. Yet, he wanted her to trust him in more. Maybe.

Maybe the bet wasn't silly. Maybe fate had intervened when he was most cocky, thinking he could simply gallivant through another bet and win. Maybe it was fate that he had bumped into her.

At the very least, she trusted him in this. So he would devote himself to making this the best experience for her.

"I'll give you your options then."

Her soft smile pierced his heart. She could be vulnerable. She could be sweet. He had seen it. Yet she could be fierce. She was everything he needed but didn't know he wanted in a woman. And she was here, trusting him with her body. Possibly more.

"If I give you two options, there's always a third. Any time you want to stop, just say it."

She nodded.

"First option," he said, pointing toward the fireplace, "chaise or bed?"

"Chaise."

He led her by the hand and sunk into the chaise. The tent in his breeches already jutting upward to greet her.

"Come," he tugged her wrist and positioned her to straddle him. As she did, what little fabric she had pooled around her hips, and he could see her bare thighs. His hands stroked her smooth skin and squeezed. "God, you're beautiful. The most beautiful warrior queen I've ever seen."

She chuckled. "You've seen many then?"

"None. You're the only one."

She leaned forward and took his lips for ransom. It was not gentle. It was not the quiet calm she had been emitting. It was voracious. Her body was plied to his and then sinking down onto him. And the friction he craved soon started.

This was not at all the pace he had in mind, but if she was setting it, he was in it.

His hands dove up her back caressing her, feeling her. The closeness was heady. She was everything soft and fierce, and he couldn't stop himself from wanting more.

And then she was up on her knees, pressing her breasts against his chest, and he wanted to be wearing far fewer layers. None to be precise.

His heart was on fire. His cock was on fire. The whole house could be on fire and he wouldn't care. He needed her like he had never needed a woman before.

He pulled back. "Let me kiss you," he whispered.

"Yes," she answered and he knew she didn't understand what she was agreeing to.

"Options," he remembered aloud with a ragged breath. "Here." He pointed to her nipples then dragged his finger down to her center. "Here."

She nodded with heavy lids. "Yes," she arched upward.

With the slightest tremble, he reached up and untied her straps, letting the bodice fall. Famished, he took one of her breasts and sucked. Her moan sunk into his ears, his bones. He pushed up into her, alleviating the ache he knew they both possessed. He laved on her nipple, torturing her by pulling away and blowing a cool stream over the wet trail he had left with his tongue.

"Wesley," she moaned his name. It was too much. He had to kiss her more deeply.

"I need to kiss you," he said as he lifted her. He laid her on the carpet near enough to the fire to stay warm.

"Options," he had barely remembered to offer them. "Here," he pointed to her core again. "Or here." Her lips. Parted.

She couldn't speak but used her hand to cover her mons.

Oh God, that was the choice he wanted her to make. He wanted to taste her. He wanted to drink from her fount and worship her body.

He circled her ankles with his hands and slowly ran his palms up toward her thighs, exposing more and more of her until finally he saw her dark curls.

Kisses. All up her leg, on the side of her knee, up along and upward, inward on her thigh. He could see her chest moving up and down quicker now.

And as much as he wanted to lick her senseless, he needed her trust. He wanted absolute certainty sure that she wanted it too.

He asked permission once more to lick the cunny of his goddess.

"Yes?"

Chapter Sixteen

"Yes," she whispered hoarsely. "Please, Wesley." She could feel herself dripping wet. He answered with his tongue. There. God, he was lapping at her. The groans overtook her body. She arched her hips up into his face. Her hands were in his hair. Holding him close. She was restless. Aching.

He needed to give her what she wanted, and God, she never knew how much she would want his lips on her down there.

His tongue flicked over her once tight bud, and she nearly shouted in ecstasy.

"Yes, Wesley," was all she could manage to say.

His tongue entered her core and she had no sense of location, only a destination she wanted to reach.

"Please," she whimpered.

He withdrew his tongue and gently put a finger, then two, inside of her. Pressing, padding, circling until her destination was so close she could smell it. It smelled of sandalwood. And mint.

And then his tongue was licking rhythmically along her bud and she knew he would meet her where she wanted to go.

"Wesley," the last word from her place of origin. Her body trembled and she felt something spill out of her.

"Oh my God, Boudicca. You've given me the best drink of my life."

And he was about to stand. She didn't want him going anywhere. The thought of him leaving, even to add the slightest distance was unthinkable. She had been sated, but really, she wanted more. She needed to feel him again. She wanted to feel him in every possible way. The impossibility could be a reality if she reached for it. She need only lift her hand, or open her mouth and ask for what she wanted.

Despite her limbs being weak and heavy, she reached up to him. She knew there was more. And she wanted it. Something about him was different tonight. Fully real. Fully himself. He was only here for her. And she wanted it all. Despite everything she was falling for him. And if she was falling, she wanted her chance at fullness. She would fall hard. Even if she fell alone.

She needed to know it all.

"Options?" she asked weakly.

Astonishment prevented him from giving an answer. So she took the lead.

"This." She grazed his raging erection. "Here."

"I like that option." He smiled a wicked smile. "Are you sure?"

"Yes. Now."

He opened his falls and his cock sprang out. The ruddy head already had a glistening bead of liquid poking out. She wanted to taste him. Suck on him. But that was a wickedness that would have to wait because she wanted him inside of her. Some primal instinct had taken over, knowledgeable beyond its experience. She just knew that she wanted to trust her body.

She moaned, remembering how his fingers felt inside of her. With a lick of her lips, she asked, "Can we…now?"

He was on his elbows atop her, his mouth attached to her neck. Then down to her nipple. Then up to her mouth. She could taste herself on his tongue. It was the most erotic thing she had tasted. His arousal was pressing at her core, sliding up and down between her sensitive folds. The music of moans filled the air as his hand reached down to hold his cock and ease it into her.

This moment that she could have never predicted was actually about to happen. The duke everyone wanted, the one that hadn't given any woman a second glance, was giving himself to her. She would be a fool to think it would lead to a future together of fencing and having a family, but she couldn't help being a fool for the first time in her life. A person couldn't choose who they fell for.

His eyes were gazing into hers with something akin to adoration alongside concern. "This might hurt—"

"I want all of you, Wesley. Please." It was a plea that had more meaning than she cared to unpack in the moment. "Now." She thrust up and took him inside of her.

There was a pinch. A flash of pain, and then unspeakable pleasure. He was filling her completely. His groan met her ear, and he asked, "Are you all right?"

"Yes. More, Wesley," she said.

"Say my name again, and I'll give it to you."

"Please, Wesley."

"Uhh…" he thrust into her to the hilt. She could feel him everywhere. Her legs wrapped around him the way his scent enveloped her.

And he was moving, his own rhythm. His own pace. But a pace perfectly set by her moaning. She could feel him thickening inside of her.

His thumb found the place, her nub, and he fluttered it against her a few times, heeding her body's responses. Even though seeking his own pleasure, he was aware of her completely. Wanting her to experience her own pleasure again. He was arrogant. He was untouchable. But he was hers in this moment.

"Come all over my cock, Boudicca, just like you came in my mouth."

The words should have shocked her into retreat, but instead they propelled her forward. She wanted to meet him exactly where he was and where he was calling her to be. With him encapsulating her, she felt his strength and the power it gave her as well. "Uhhhh…" she felt her release come again. All over him.

He grunted, and with a wince he thrust into her and pulled

out. Spilling between her thighs.

She was a hot, sweaty mess. But never had she felt so natural. So whole.

Without even a moment to catch her breath, he rolled onto his side and pulled her into his embrace.

"When shall we get married?"

"Don't joke about such serious matters."

"I'm not joking. I just stole your innocence, we should marry."

"I'm not innocent. I'm a spinster. And you didn't steal anything."

"I'm glad you said that," He kissed her nose. "Not the spinster part. The stealing part. I gave you options, and you chose the way forward. Now I'm giving you another option. Marriage."

"I thought I wasn't a lady. Why are you doing the honorable thing right now?"

"It's not about honor. It's about…connection. I've never felt this way before. It's never been this good." He kissed her collarbone. "I know I'll never have enough of you. Besides, if everything else fails, we'll always have fencing."

"If everything else fails, I'll slash you to death using my rapier."

He laughed. "Then not everything else will fail. We could have a wonderful life. You intrigue me."

Intrigue was more the stuff of mysteries than love. It wasn't as romantic as one would hope for a proposal. But it wasn't altogether unromantic.

He cupped her chin and asked, "What do I need to do? Bring you chocolates again?"

"You may always bring me chocolates."

"I shall bring you pale pink peonies, chocolates, and all the ices you desire."

He was smiling. A large, guileless smile. As if he really did want to marry her. As if he weren't just doing the honorable thing.

It wasn't love. At least, not that she could detect. But her sisters had made some observations, so it wasn't entirely implausible…

"I need time to think."

"Take all the time you want."

She sighed in relief.

"Wait. I take that back. Take some time. One and a half days at most, if it pleases you."

It did not please her. "Why one and a half days?"

"I'd like to know your answer before the fencing tournament."

"Why is that?"

"It will either fuel me in anger or fuel me in delight."

A notable avoidance of the word love was not unappreciated.

He continued, "What would be the worst scenario is if I'm still in limbo awaiting your answer during the tournament. Liminal space is the least desirable space by the human race."

"Ah…so it all comes down to fencing. I can't say I disapprove of that sentiment. I shall give you my answer before the tournament."

It was a good thing that Wesley had given her a deadline, else she could have spent countless days and weeks mulling over his question.

As it was, she knew the next day and a half were going to require every ounce of mental and emotional fortitude she possessed. So it was unfortunate that the man lying beside her left her so weak in the knees. That meant, first thing tomorrow, it would be time to rally the troops.

BEFORE BREAKFAST, BOUDICCA had messages sent to her sisters to meet in her room. Joan and Nobi rushed in with concern wrought on their faces, while Mimi sauntered in with a smile.

"So…did you change?" Mimi asked.

Boudicca blushed.

"Good. So I was right?"

"Right about what?" the other two asked.

"The duke was here last night."

"Oh my God, Mimi. Don't you think that's news for me to share?"

"He was here?" Mimi gasped. "Oh my God, oh my God, I was right?"

"You just said that," Boudicca rolled her eyes.

"Yes, but I didn't think it. It was a ploy to see if you would divulge the truth. And then you did. And he did come. And I was right."

How annoying to have young sisters who were right at the worst possible times.

"Fine." Boudicca gestured for everyone to sit down. Then she turned and faced them. "I don't know how else to say it. Wesley was here last night and he proposed."

"Oh. My. God. You're going to marry a duke?" Mimi was all but shouting.

"Will you please be quiet? Everyone will hear."

"The dare worked?" Mimi was beside herself. "I can't believe it. I can't believe it."

"Well, believe it, dear sister," Boudicca said.

She repeated in a hushed whisper, "You're going to marry a duke."

"Botheration. Not that part. The part about him being here. He came here last night."

Mimi pointed to the window with a cocked brow.

"Yes, through the window," Boudicca muttered. "But I didn't say yes."

"You turned him away?"

"Oh my God, Mimi, are you even listening? He came in. He was here. We made…" she blushed as she waved her arm to the fireplace.

"You made fire."

"Yes, Mimi. We made fire." She had never been sarcastic with her sisters before. She was patient. Prim. Proper. Responsible. Only…she wasn't all of that all of the time. And she was becoming less so of it more of the time. If that made sense…It was too much. The exasperation. The emotion. Now she actually had to say the words aloud to her younger, impressionable sisters who were about to set off on their own duke dares.

Joan stepped in, laying a hand on Mimi to quiet whatever garble was about to come out of her mouth. "So he was here." She waved her hand around the fireplace where Boudicca had gestured. "And he proposed?"

"But I didn't accept his proposal."

Joan nodded silently.

"Why didn't you accept?" Mimi asked.

"I'm sure she has her reasons," Nobi said. "Don't you?" It was almost a plea.

"If only I knew…" Boudicca sighed.

"He knows you. Better than any man ever has. You've let him in. That means something." Mimi said.

"He likes you, though I think it's more than like. And it could grow into love," Joan was now on board with the youngest.

"Do I want to take that gamble though? Do I not deserve love? Shouldn't I wait until the man I love is humble enough, happy enough, courageous enough to love me in return?"

"Yes."

"Well, shouldn't I?"

"Yes." Joan repeated. "You absolutely do deserve that. And if you don't think it's with Wesley, then say no. Just know that even for the average man it's a challenge to decipher their own feelings. Never mind one as haughty as Wesley. So yes, it's a gamble. But it's a gamble either way."

And therein lay the problem. Life without love, alongside a man. Life without love, alone. Neither option looked great.

And it wasn't until later that she realized she had referred to Wesley as the man she loved.

CHAPTER SEVENTEEN

THE TITTERS OF gossip greeted Boudicca and her sisters upon being announced at Countess Linsgate's ball. The garden party news was widespread. The handsome, powerful Duke of Baskim, the *ton*'s most selective bachelor, had set his sights on someone. Her.

And though her heart was swarming with feelings, she maintained her composure and led her sisters to the dance floor. It seemed scandalous to be sans chaperone now, when only a few days ago, no one had batted an eyelash at the spinster.

Hundreds of eyes followed her every movement. Watching for what? Something incriminating? Some piece of evidence as to why—why on God's green earth—he had chosen her? What was so special about her? Everyone wanted to know. Hell, she wanted to know, too. But she was having a bit of trouble suppressing the grin vying for purchase on her face.

Maybe she had found someone who liked her for her full self. As her sisters had said, he knew more about her than any man, and he made the most effort with her.

She thought back to her early demands of flowers, chocolate, and a gift. A woman had to have standards, even if they were outrageous. And how she had pushed him by ordering an exorbitant number of ices…well, she hadn't backed down and neither had he. It had led to their bouts on the piste, and she couldn't be happier.

Except she could be.

Suddenly, the manly source of all her current vexation was at her side. "Before the dance requests start flooding in, I must insist that you save a waltz for me. The first one is my preference."

"Of course, Your Grace." She took the dance card dangling on her wrist, something she hadn't had any use for of late, and she wrote his name down. "I dare say it's a wise act to reserve your dance. With all my suitors, you might have missed your chance otherwise."

"You jest, but I'm sure more than a few eyes have been opened this evening. I saw the crowds observing your entrance. And before you say it could have been your sisters, I must interject. I was studying them while they studied you. So in this case, I know my evaluation is correct."

With that, he kissed her hand and left.

And true to his prediction, her card filled up, and thankfully before Lord Tamely was able to snare her into a dance. He had backed down over the years, but with all the attention she was receiving tonight, she had no doubt he would toss his hat in the ring. Apparently, all a spinster needed was the attention of a duke to bring her into light. The dances were a delight. She twirled, and smiled. Laughed and curtsied. It was the perfect evening. Even some of the conversations hadn't been altogether tedious.

But tedious did not compare to elation. Wesley was beside her again, arm extended, inviting her to dance. A waltz with him. Their relationship (if she was brave enough to call it that) was public. Everyone would see. Everyone would know. The whisper of gossip from the garden party would surely be reignited after this dance.

None of that was on her mind though. All that she perceived was the warmth of his fingers through her gloves. The heat from his eyes on her lips. And then the light pressure of his hand along her back as he swirled her onto the dance floor. Nothing existed outside of the dance. Beyond the depth of his gaze, there were no other eyes. The music enveloped them in a cloud of bliss.

He was strong. He was sure of himself. He knew what he wanted in life, and he went after it. No matter what she threw at him. No matter how she lunged at him, he had taken the hit. Lost the point. Failed to win. Yet was determined to persevere. And how a man did one thing was often how he did many things. Perhaps even everything.

She had seen his weakness, and he was not a man to reveal that kind of defect. He wanted to win, and he wanted everyone to see that. It was pride, to be sure, but it was dignity. It was self-respect. And she wanted that for him. And she wanted it even more for herself. Her dreams to open a fencing academy would be possible with him. She could share her future with him tonight, and if he agreed to it, then she would marry him.

Because in her heart, she knew. This was the man she wanted. This was the man she could allow herself to envision a future with.

He liked her. He was attentive. And as her sisters had encouraged, it could turn to love. She would be a fool to outright reject his proposal when a very bright and happy future could await them both.

There was no exchange of words. Only his soft eyes languidly perusing her face. It was the zenith of intimacy. To be content in silence. More than content, absolutely filled. She had only ever felt this way with him. With that knowledge and acceptance of her feelings, she was set on her answer.

The waltz was ending, so she rushed to whisper, "I'll tell you my answer tonight."

His smile melted her heart. And somehow she knew that she hadn't been alone in her feelings during the waltz.

Her next dance was with Samuel, Duke of Cadmore. When he approached, Wesley was loathe to give her up.

"On your best behavior, Cadmore."

Samuel only laughed. He had a coy smile on his face and a light but unyielding grip on her fingers. And she couldn't help the prickling sensation all along her neck. Wesley was watching them more closely than his casual observations of her other partners. Intriguing.

"You have a bevy of fine partners this evening, Lady Boudicca."

"Yes, it's quite irregular." There was no point in claiming otherwise. Everyone had known of her spinster status prior to the garden party.

"You have your pick it would seem."

"So it would seem." She answered trepidatiously.

"Ah…but then nothing is as it seems, is it?"

"Quite."

He laughed. "You have nothing to say to that? Come now. I've heard that you like to spar."

Wesley wouldn't have told people about her secret, would he?

"Verbally," Samuel added in a dry tone.

"Perhaps I do, with the right opponent."

"I'm wounded."

There was no maliciousness that she could detect, but there was something askew in his questions. Almost as if he were hinting at a secret.

"I hadn't intended to wound you, Your Grace," Boudicca said, wanting to tread carefully, but also keep the conversation open.

"Those are sometimes the deepest cuts. The unintentional ones."

"I rather doubt this is one of those times," she said wryly.

"Perhaps you are right. I do suppose it has to be with the right opponent." He smiled.

"Touche." His jest seemed to be made in good faith, not in any way mocking.

"Our time is coming to a close soon, so I shall just leave you with a single word."

He did have a secret. It was clear now. But leaving her with a word? For what purpose? To what end? And what was the word going to be? How would she know if she interpreted it correctly?

A million questions flew through her mind, none of them landing, all of them in a flock, banding together.

And then he dropped a single word. It was the one word she had been plagued with since her time with the duke began. It was, perhaps, the only word the Duke of Cadmore could have voiced that would have thrown her for such a loop as it did.

"Motive."

"I SAW YOUR dance with Samuel, Duke of Cadmore." Wesley caught up to her just before it was time to go in for dinner.

"Yes."

"You looked like you were enjoying yourself."

"Did I? That's good to hear because I don't like him, and I wasn't sure I was disguising it very well."

"Nobody likes him."

"He's your friend, isn't he?"

"We put up with him." He shrugged.

A dance ago, she was absolutely sure of her decision. Now observing him with a cagey expression, she had regressed. She wanted to shrug it off similarly to how he had just done. Perhaps the best approach was the direct one. That was her modus operandi, why change it?

"Samuel mentioned something."

"Oh?" Wesley's eye flickered across the crowd, neglecting to give her his full attention.

"Yes, it was quite off-putting."

His eyes kept scanning, as discreetly as he could.

"Surreptitious, one might say."

The furtive glances ceased, and his eyes narrowed in reaction to her. "He was being cryptic? About what?"

"Isn't that the point in a secret? One party doesn't know what the other does."

He nodded. "So what did he say?"

"He said—"

"Oh there you are, Your Grace." Countess Linsgate cooed. "I believe you're escorting me in for dinner this evening." She wrapped her tentacles around his arm and pulled him toward the doors.

It would have to wait, but she would tell him. There was nothing worse than secrets in a relationship. She would have to make a point to bring that up before accepting his proposal.

It took a few moments for everyone to find their seats. In the commotion, Joan found her and whispered. "What's going on?"

"Botheration. Has everyone noticed?" Momentarily she forgot that her actions were now under fastidious scrutiny, being the duke's object of affection.

"Put a smile on. No, not that big. Tone it down a touch. Yes, that's perfect." Joan patted her arm. "I doubt anyone else would recognize your disquiet, but I'm your sister. I know your facial expressions."

"Thank you."

"Is everything all right?"

"It will be. I hope."

"You are a strong, capable woman, Boudicca. Whatever it is, you can handle it. And if for any reason you can't, we're all here for you." Joan, the quiet one, the most reserved of all four daughters, was soft-spoken but poignant, and Boudicca couldn't have been happier to have her.

Zenobia was quickly at her side with Artemisia, a flash of consternation on their faces, swiftly replaced with plastered smiles.

"What did he do?" Nobi ground out through clenched teeth. Her soft demeanor was a facade. She was likely the fiercest of them all. The makings of her ferocity were that of a mother bear with her cubs, and if anyone were to hurt the one she loved, there would be a bloody price to pay.

Boudicca's eyes misted, but it was not the time or place for displays of emotion.

"He didn't do anything. I don't think. Or maybe, not yet." It was a confuffled mess in her mind as to whether or not he had done anything. She didn't want to presume guilt without knowing the facts.

"That sounds like he did something," Mimi's smile was less plasterful than the others. She was not one to easily hide herself.

"It's all right."

"Bodi—"

"Mimi, it's all right. I'll rally the troops if I need to. I know you're here for me."

"We are," the three chorused.

"I know. And I love you all for it. Now let's eat before someone asks where the four Wells sisters are."

She quickly squeezed her sisters' hands and then they found their seats. She knew she was blessed to have such a caring and supportive family, and that knowledge bolstered her confidence.

Soon conversation was flowing and Boudicca was almost diverted enough to forget her current plight. Until a subtle trill of a laugh caused her to catch sight of Lady Simone's hand on Wesley's forearm.

What the deuce was she laughing at? And didn't she know women weren't supposed to laugh that loudly in public? Especially in mixed company.

Then she saw Lady Simone flutter her long eyelashes at Wesley and moue her lips, feigning admonishment.

The duke flirting at dinner. The duke's seemingly impulsive decision to attend the garden party. The duke's peculiar behavior on Rotten Row. All three instances involved Lady Simone. It couldn't be a coincidence, could it? He didn't seem to have a tendre for her, for he had labeled her a gossip. Almost disdainfully so. But the way he was saying things to make her laugh...and the way she was laughing at everything...He wasn't that funny.

Oh Lord, if there hadn't been all these people around she

would have thrown her potatoes at the woman. However, if there hadn't been all these people around, perhaps Lady Simone wouldn't be acting so flirtatiously. Food for thought, it was.

All the same, did Wesley have to leave his arm on the table for all and sundry to fondle? Or was he the type of man to dally with other women when in a relationship? That would not do. Another point to bring up before she gave him her answer. The list of stipulations was growing.

If she waited any longer to give her answer, she would have to start writing the list down.

Chapter Eighteen

After her observations of Lady Simone's coquettish ways, she lost track of the conversations around her, nodding when it seemed appropriate and regurgitating a few select phrases such as, *Do you really think so?* and *Could it be?* It was sufficient to satisfy the people sitting beside her. Though it hardly did anything to assuage the gnawing feeling in her gut. She couldn't remember ever feeling such a twisting in her stomach. As though someone were kneading bread in there. It was an awful feeling. Awful, more so, because she had to admit that this feeling was…jealousy. And she was not a jealous person.

But it wasn't simple jealousy, it was jealousy with a small degree of uncertainty. She didn't know exactly where Wesley's affections laid. Yes, he had proposed, but he had never said he loved her. Made a point in fact to point out what their marriage would be like and why it was beneficial to them both. Did she even have a right to be jealous for someone's nonexistent affections? Or unstated affections?

Jealousy was certainly complicating matters in her mind, so when the guests were dismissed, she made a quick getaway to take some fresh air.

Just before she reached the door, Nobi met her.

"Where are you going?"

"I just need a moment to clear my head with some fresh air."

"Shall I join you?"

"Thank you, but no. I want to be alone." She hesitated. It was a fortunate coincidence to run into Zenobia. Of all the sisters, she knew her own feelings best. After all, she had been in love with Christopher forever. "Nobi, how do you know your feelings? How do you know to trust them?"

"There's no perfect answer to that one unfortunately. You can't help your feelings. But you can manage them. You can let them control you, or you can control them. I've found the best thing for me is to accept a feeling and not fight it. That way it passes through me and runs its course. If it doesn't pass through, then I have to find out why. Is it meant to stay?" she looked across the room, her eyes immediately finding Chris. "Or am I meant to move on? I still don't know."

"How did you know you loved him?"

"It's impossible to describe. I just…I just want what's best for him. Even if it's not me."

That sounded torturous. How did Zenobia live with such an ache in her heart?

"Don't worry about me." A sardonic smile curved her lips. It was genuine and reassuring. "I'm making my plan to snare him, and then I'll have my answer one way or the other. Worry about yourself right now. I know you're in the middle of something life-changing, Bodi. Just remember that it's your life. No one can live it for you. It's yours to feel. Only yours to live."

She squeezed Zenobia's hand.

"I'll let you go, but if you need to leave, just remember our code word," she winked as she said it. "We'll whisk you out of here before anyone's the wiser."

With that safeguard in place, she stepped out onto one of the terraces and breathed in the light chill. What a mess she had found herself in. To accept Wesley's proposal or not…under what conditions…and would he agree to all of them. If he loved—liked—her enough, hopefully he would give his assent. As long as he complied (not really his nature, but so far his way of being with her at least indicated that he was capable of doing so), she could envision a happy future together. She could finally be her full self to the world. Her heart dipped in excitement at the mere thought to be able to help other young girls find a way to be themselves.

Boudicca slid her hands along the balustrade. The night sky was lit by the moon and a few puffs of clouds. It was the perfect space to think with no one—

"I do say you need to catch us up on everything, Wesley."

Botheration! Multiple male voices that she was not ready for. She stole behind the open terrace door and crushed herself against the exterior wall of the manor, hoping they wouldn't see her. If perchance they did, she would say she needed fresh air…and…had stopped to smell…the—erm…wisteria. Obviously, she prayed it would not come to that.

She could hear everything the men were saying. Even the thud of a hand smacking Wesley on the back.

"What a crush," someone said.

"Yes. I saw you both danced with Lady Boudicca," another said.

"Yes, about that, Samuel…" Wesley started to say.

"Yes about that. What's going on with Lady Boudicca?" A voice asked.

"Precisely my thoughts indeed. It seems like you're taking it all quite seriously." That sounded like Samuel, but she couldn't be sure. She had only danced a short time with him.

"It is serious."

The men laughed.

"Trust you to be so grave about love."

"It's marriage," Wesley clarified. And the clarity was a shard of glass in her heart. If he was only saying that to save face with his male companions, it was still a cut, but not so deep. But she didn't perceive him as the type to kowtow to his friends.

"It's a proposal." The maybe-Samuel voice said. "That's what the bet was. Bump into her. Court her. Propose."

Bet?

If the night sky had been dark before, it was black now. Her vision blurred. Her heart dropped to her slippers. Thunder rolled in her ears, fuzzing the rest of the chatter. She didn't hear any more of it. It was all just a bet? By The Betting Buddies? Bumping into her was planned? That first night at the ball? That's why he endured their outrageous courtship? He *had* to stick it out? *That's* why he proposed? What the hell was going on?

Oh my God. It was so much worse than anything she had imagined. He could have been after *some* appealing attribute of hers, something. Anything. Status. Fortune. Beauty. She winced. No. He was after none of it. He was pursuing *her* for no reason. A bet. A deuced, damn bet.

She wanted to step out from behind the door and thrash him. She wanted to call him out and duel. She wanted to hurt him the way he had just hollowed her out. She would never allow herself to hope again.

But there was no fire in her spirit to do any of that. Instead, she smoothed her skirts, and stepped out from behind the door.

Without looking at any of them except Wesley, she raised a hand to quiet their murmured surprise.

Her eyes seared into him. She didn't give any credence to the disbelief and—was that pain?—in his eyes.

There was only thing to do. Only one word to speak. It wasn't a clue. It wasn't a secret. Nothing was hidden anymore. It was the godawful, plain, ugly truth.

"No."

WITH THE CODE word, *Bucephalus*, Boudicca's sisters asked no questions but hurried her home. It wasn't until they were seated in her room and gathered on her bed did they wait expectantly for a coze on what had happened. None of them suffered a weak constitution, but if Boudicca was using their highest emergency code word, they all knew something of great proportions had happened.

Surprisingly Joan, not Mimi, broke the silence. "No one's had to use that code word since…" Her eyes flitted around the sororal circle.

"Since that bastard tried to sneak Boudicca off into the gardens?"

"Mimi, language," Nobi chided.

"Well, he was one. The set down was as accurate when I said it then as it is now."

"You're lucky no one heard you back then," Nobi said.

"Not for lack of trying," Mimi smirked.

Boudicca let her sisters banter while she collected her thoughts. A thousand thoughts of fluff had flown through her briarbush of a mind, and now the trapped fuzz was impossible to see through.

It was all fake. It was all a lie. She had been duped. He was just like every other man. But a million times worse. Her heart had not stopped racing. A pulse that was impossible to sustain. It was wearing on her nerves and draining her energy. She felt a fool to allow her heart to trust him. Him. Of all dukes. The most particular duke of them all. Why had she thought that there was something special about her?

No, she knew her worth. Why had she thought that he was something special to notice her worth when all men had ulterior motives? Why should she feel down about herself when he was the one who had been lying?

"Boudicca?" Joan rubbed her forearm. "Are you all right?"

"I'm fine." She didn't want their pity.

"What can we do to make that true?" Joan asked. "What…what did he do?"

She opened her mouth to dismiss their concern but clamped her jaw shut. Why should she cover his actions?

"It was all a lie." Traitorously, the corners of her eyes stung, and she shrugged in an attempt to will them away. "It was a bet."

"What was a bet?" Nobi asked.

"Me." A couple of tears spilled out. "I was the bet. None of it was real."

"You can't say that. We saw the way he looked at you," Mimi said.

"Whatever you saw was fake. He might be a damn good actor, but I can assure you it was all an act."

"But he proposed? Why would anyone offer a betrothal to win a bet? It makes no sense," Mimi pondered.

"I don't understand it. I won't pretend to either. All I know is what I heard. I'm the butt of their joke."

"Who?" Mimi demanded with fire in her eyes.

"It doesn't matter."

"Like hell it doesn't matter. And don't tell me to watch my language," she warned her sisters.

"I wasn't going to." Nobi had a similar fire gleaming in her eyes. "If someone's hurt our sister, we're going to make him pay."

"That's right," Joan added.

"It's not your fight, my dear sisters. I don't know how, but I'll come out stronger for this."

Mimi looked downright devilish as she said, "I know exactly how you're going to make him pay, and I won't take no for an answer."

"What are you talking about, Mimi?"

"The fencing tournament," she said proudly. "You're going to enter it. And you're going to beat him in front of everyone."

"I can't do that," Boudicca said.

"Didn't you say you beat him when you practiced here together?" Joan asked.

"That's different."

"How? If you're skilled enough to best him here, you can beat him anywhere," Nobi said.

"I do believe that's true. Though it pained Wesley to admit it, he conceded that I was the better fencer."

"There you have it," Mimi said.

"That's not the issue."

"What is?" Joan asked.

"Only men are eligible to enter that fencing competition. You all know that."

Mimi blew a raspberry with her lips. "Pffff...that's the easy part, Bodi. We'll make up a name for you, you'll change in your own space and leave your mask in place whenever you're in public. Easy."

"I wouldn't say easy—" Joan started.

Mimi glared at Joan. "It is easy. And it is the best way for Bodi to get revenge. Don't you all agree? She can beat him. And he would be humiliated in front of everyone."

"I suppose..." Joan said. "Do we really want to see him humiliated?"

"Annihilated would be better," Mimi threatened.

"That doesn't sound very loving," Boudicca said.

"Loving? What has he done?" Mimi scoffed, then muttered, "The bastard."

"He's not—"

"Whatever. This is about revenge. Love's first cousin. They're related. Trust me. And nothing tests a relationship better than familial ties."

"Mimi might be bloodthirsty," Nobi jumped in, "but I think her plan is the best thing to do."

"See?"

"But"—Nobi put her hand up to stay Mimi's comments—"I think her plan is best for a different reason." She turned to Boudicca. "This is your dream, Bodi. Don't let a man get in the way. Whatever he did, and to be honest, I'm not sure that whatever bet he may have had didn't turn into some real feelings for him. I know. It's hard to believe, but I saw the way he looked at you. Especially during your dance tonight. I think his heart may have been involved. But that's not important for us to decide. That's only for you to determine. And if you don't want to discuss it with him, I respect your decision. However, I do believe you should enter the competition and win. Beat every man you match up against. And then, when the tournament is over, reveal yourself. If you want. You'll have created a scandal, without doubt. But there will also be no doubt in anyone's mind should they wonder who to hire as a fencing tutor for their daughter."

"I agree," Joan said. "You should do it."

"I can't do it. None of you will be able to find a match, let alone the dukes we all agreed to snare."

"We accept the consequences," Mimi said, with a flip of her hand, "all of them. And if the dares are meant to be, we'll still find a way to accomplish them. We have, none of us, backed down from a challenge."

"True," Nobi added. "We stand with you. Whatever you decide."

CHAPTER NINETEEN

*N*O.
NO.
NO.

IT rang through Wesley's ears. No matter how much he drank, he couldn't drown those two tenacious bastards. N, the wily sod couldn't decide which way he was going up or down, so he couldn't be caught. And O, the spurious cad. Just a giant hole. One that Wesley felt he was sinking into. How could two sneaky little letters pack such a blow? His sternum hurt. Why did his sternum hurt?

No. No. No. He reviled the word, especially when he heard it blast from her lips. It was one of the most powerful words in the English language. It was the word he should have said when Samuel asked him if he wanted to go out carousing after the ball. It was the word he should have said when the second bottle of whiskey was cracked open. It was the word he should have said when the Betting Buddies started a game of piquet. Thank God he had the presence of mind to say it when the buxom wench came and offered for him.

That was the only part of the evening he knew he wouldn't regret. He had said no. And then he had said yes to a few more drinks. Thus, him cradling his head on the table.

Samuel and James were still swapping coins over another card game. White's was crowded, as if all the gentlemen from the ball had trickled over to the club after the festivities but before heading home. He only hoped that none of them wanted to have a chitchat. He was in no mood to make small talk. Large talk. Or any kind of medium talk.

After Boudicca had left the four of them on the terrace, he hadn't said much. Other than to accept their invitation to go out, so long as there would be drinking, he was in. The gambling had been a nice bonus, well, actually, it had been a slight drain on his cash, but the game was worth it. If only to be distracted for a short time.

If he went home, he knew what would greet him. His bed. Which he'd been avoiding. But even a restless sleep on the settee meant dreams. And his dreams meant Boudicca. He did not want to dream of her tonight. Better to avoid that for as long as possible. So he sat in his club in an awkward predicament. He neither wanted to be alone with his thoughts, nor did he want to talk.

"This isn't like you, Wesley," Christopher sank into the seat beside him where he had been temporarily observing the room.

"Saxby, really, now isn't the time for chastisement," Wesley mumbled.

"What would I be chastising you about?"

"Drinking. Betting. To name a couple." Wesley lifted his head enough to peer out through bleary eyes.

Chris raised his glass in mockery. "No judgment here. Perchance, what betting are you referring to though? The piquet? Or..."

"Or." Wesley declared.

"Well, in that case...yes, it seems you're rather bollocks deep in that one."

"Thanks for letting me know, you dolt."

"Pleasure."

Wesley dropped his head to the table, missing his forearm. Thwack!

"She'd probably say that you deserved that."

"She would, wouldn't she?" Wesley chuckled.

"How are you planning to get her back?"

"I'm not."

"Really? The great Duke of Baskim is rolling over and accepting defeat over one measly little setback?"

"I wouldn't call it measly."

"And you would call it…?"

"Rather devastating, really."

"Hmmm…" Chris hummed loudly enough for Wesley to be more than a little irked.

"What, pray tell, are you humming so obnoxiously about?"

"Just never heard you refer to something as devastating before. Might you be alluding to the state of your heart?"

At that Wesley's head whipped up. Which, in hindsight, was a terrible miscalculation of his control on his balance. His head sloshed to one side, pulling him nearly off the chair, and then in an overcorrection, he swung it the opposite direction, nearly colliding with Chris' chest.

"Wait, just a minute." He held up a finger. Or two, he wasn't sure. "I'm not drinking for…lost love." He sputtered. "I'm drinking because I lost the bet."

"Right."

"I despise losing."

"Right."

"I'm a competitor."

"You don't have to tell me that."

"And I'll not rest until I win."

"I completely agree."

"Speaking of which, I've got to get home now and abed. Tomorrow I must continue my training. I still have a fencing tournament to win."

"Of course you do," Chris just nodded.

The cursed knave was at the height of his patronizing, but all Wesley could say in return was the startlingly eloquent, "I do."

To which Chris reached the apex of his sarcasm, "Right."

Was he going to sit there all night and listen to this scapegrace? Or was he going to do something about his situation? Wesley was not the kind to drink his sorrows away. What sorrows? He was not the kind to lament and wallow in anguish. He was a man of action. And just because one gorgeous blonde-haired-rapier-wielding intoxicating gel had...had...had gotten under his skin (a little), did not mean he would succumb to disheartenment.

What was he if he was not a worthy competitor? He still had a goal to reach. Forget Boudicca and her tempting lips and full breasts. She could have her secret gymnasium of glory. He had more important things to do. To be. To have. He had to win.

Wesley stood up. Slowly. "Now,"—he bowed, and in his most mockingest of tones, chirped—"be a dear and show me the way out, you lout."

Wesley didn't make it more than a few steps without Chris' help. In fact, James ended up under one of his armpits, and Chris under the other. Samuel, of course, laughing behind them all the way home.

Once at his residence, they handed him over to the butler and some footmen with the profound parting words that no man heeded, "Don't do anything stupid."

Of course, he was home, what stupid could he really do? He wasn't about to make his way over to her house just before dawn, lift her brocade counterpane, and climb into her warm bed with her. He recalled her sounds. Her silky locks. The way his fingers wanted to get lost in them. He could smell her soft rose scent. How had he never named her scent until now? The fragrance was inebriating. He shouldn't have had to drink a drop tonight. He could have just conjured her scent and lost his senses to her. And her in her bed.

No, that bed was for...

Ugh. He groaned.

He did not want to say the words. If it wasn't him in her bed, eventually it would be another...man. He ground his teeth in frustration. His normally rigid spine was hunched over as the footmen aided his ascent up the stairs.

To his bedchambers. The dreaded den of dreams. Though not to his bed. He fell asleep on the settee.

Delaying the inevitable, he slowly shirked out of his clothing and then laid to rest with his most useless prayer to date. *Please don't let me dream of her.*

LEADING UP TO the tournament, Wesley had trained every day. Hard. Servants that were otherwise content to be in his employ steered clear of him. They took turns bringing him trays of food and reassured each other that his growling would pass. Surely, a man with a calm demeanor (until this week) would not turn into a permanent monster. Surely, the smashed vase out of anger was a onetime occurrence. Surely, he would not be so demanding as to have nine flavors of ice provided at a random dinner, again. Surely.

The worst of it befell Wesley's poor valet though. The first day he had shaved Wesley, he had missed a hair on his chin. Wesley shouted obscenities. The second day, his valet had paid extra attention to the chin area and had missed a couple of hairs under Wesley's jawline. More obscenities and water on the floor. The next time the valet came to shave he had a slight tremble to his hand, and fate of all fates, had nicked his volcanic employer. The vulgarities lasted an hour. Wesley hadn't ceased his mutterings until breakfast forced him to stuff food into his mouth. And even then he had grumbled a couple of times. The fourth day the valet's hand trembled so badly that Wesley took the damn razor from him and attended to his own face. The valet had winced, but the grimace was followed by an obvious sigh of relief.

"If you can't get it right, I'll do it myself," Wesley had said. "Or I'll find someone who can." The valet was loyal though, as were they all to their master. And the decision to ride it out had been unanimous among Wesley's staff. He knew this because he had overheard a couple of them discussing *His Grace's foul temper of late.* Their grumbling only led to more grumbling from him. It would pass, though. As soon as he won this damn fencing tournament and bested Samuel. That's what he needed right now. He needed a win. He needed to sleep in his own damn bed.

He needed a breakthrough. A breakthrough from the fencing match in his head. Only two thoughts playing tag in his mind. *No.* And *Don't come home until you win.* A more formidable tag-team foe he had yet to encounter: the woman he now sought and the father he had once fought.

The fencing match in his head was hopeless, so he turned his thoughts to more controllable events. The tournament was to last two days. The first day had played out so that the best of the best would make it to day two. A fencer had to score thirty points to pass round one. There were matches all day long for each fencer to achieve their high score.

Only eight men had made it to day two. Day two was set up in pools. If Wesley won his first round, he would likely be up against Lord Tamely, the cheater. Since the poor sod Tamely was up against first was new, he probably didn't know to watch for Tamely's tricks. Samuel would win his pool, and then Wesley and Samuel would meet in the finals.

It was day two, and the auditorium was full of male spectators, most of them were betting on the winners of each pool and the overall winner of the tournament. Much money would exchange hands. He breathed in the scent of sweaty men. Manly men. Sweaty, manly men doing manly activities. No women allowed. No rose-scented (or otherwise-scented) females here. This was where he needed to be, if the tight churning in his gut was any indication.

The matches for day two were timed for a single audience, which meant everyone was able to see every fencer. As predicted, Wesley and Samuel both won their first matches. Also as predicted, Lord Tamely won his match. With cheating. The crowd had booed, but nothing was done. Wesley pitied his opponent though. Without the cheating, he was sure to have won. There was something about his movements, a flare, a dexterity he had rarely seen the likes of. The only thing to be done in a match against Tamely was to eschew his signature trip and strike more.

Anyone who had witnessed the first tournament would be privy to Tamely's move. Or at least the gossip surrounding it. His matchup must have been from outside of London not to have heard or seen it. He didn't seem the type to not be able to deflect such a simple move if he had the foreknowledge of it.

But Wesley shook the odd thoughts from his mind. They were not pertinent to his own imminent win.

The time had come for the final match. The match for *the win*. Wesley hadn't been able to execute Boudicca's signature move, just as she had forewarned him, but he had learned quite a few maneuvers from her that he knew would catch Samuel off guard.

Within a minute of stepping onto the piste, Wesley knew the win was his. The first lunge, attack, low inside. It was too easy.

After that first point, Samuel asked nonchalantly, "Who have you been training with?"

The question made Wesley consider that perhaps his body had picked up more from Boudicca than he had originally thought.

The referee made the calls to reposition and commence, and Wesley was about to advance-lunge when his mask fell from his face. What atrocious timing. Damn mask. He had a match to win. He didn't need to deal with this.

He moved to continue the match, but the referee raised his hands.

Immediately, the bout was paused while the referee insisted that Wesley return to the change room to retrieve his other mask.

When he made his way down the corridor though, he must

have opened the wrong door because instead of finding it empty, he discovered the most peculiar sight. But more peculiar than the sight was the scent that greeted him. Roses.

Chapter Twenty

Boudicca sat in the change room, in full gear save her mask, replaying the match over and over in her head. How had she tripped over her own feet? And not just once, but twice. She had never in all her years of fencing done that before, let alone two times in one bout. She was quick on her feet. Agility was one of her strengths. Yet, the referee had made the calls. The crowd booed at her poor performance, hoping for a better competitor. How had she ever thought she could compete in a man's world? It was a different world, entirely.

She couldn't shake it. It was impossible to discern if she had allowed the stress of the event to get to her, or if she had allowed her emotions to eat away at her. Whatever it was, it was something deep in her gut that would not leave her alone.

Her initial reaction to the calls of Tamely's point gained was that he cheated. She knew him as a knave. It only made sense that he would be a knave off and on the piste. Not only that though, she was *sure* she had tripped over his foot, not her own. But for so many reasons, she didn't want to contradict the referee. One, she was a woman and didn't want to voice anything for fear of being found out too early that she was female and shouldn't be competing anyway. Two, she didn't want to call him out, as in for an actual duel. His honor was at risk, and she was in no need of a match to the death. Three, it seemed as though everyone accepted the call, so perhaps she had mistaken her own movements somehow.

She had made it to day two of the tournament. There was that as an accomplishment. She sighed. Not one to be a sore loser, she was ashamed at how defeated she felt. Perhaps the extra sting came from losing to Lord Tamely. At least she knew she had beat him off the piste. He hadn't gotten his way with her there.

But then there was another thought. A sinking, pitiable thought. Perhaps she had overblown in her own mind her level of skill.

If she wasn't in such a disheartened state, she would have been watching the final match between Samuel and Wesley from the perimeter of the room. Hidden, but able to observe. She would likely never get the chance again.

But she couldn't bring herself to watch because she knew in her heart she would be cheering for Wesley to win. And that would be gut-wrenching. She wanted to despise him. She wanted to best him. But this awful niggling part of her still wanted the best for him.

They were competitors. She knew what it meant to him to win, especially against someone he had recently lost to. In order to increase his odds of triumph, he had humbled himself enough to take training from a woman for god's sake. It was hard to look back at their time together. It was almost as if she could see everything in muted color. All the moments he had stuck around just to get one step closer to winning his outlandish bet were a dreary drab gray in her eyes.

But if she was being honest with herself, there were some bright memories as well, full of pistachio green ice, blood red cut, smooth peach skin. Lots of exposed skin. Her face grew warm. How could a person think they both loved and hated someone at the same time? Why wouldn't her heart just listen to her mind? For that to happen, she supposed, she had to know what her mind was thinking. And all her thoughts regarding Wesley and fencing were now a jumbled mess.

Ugh. She sat with her mask in hand, rolling it around her

palm. She should be proud that she tried. And proud that she made it as far as she did. A person could never earn a point by sitting out.

🔥

WESLEY STOOD, GAPING, at Boudicca in her gear. Obviously she had been competing. In fact, it was so obvious now that he stopped to actually open his mind and reflect on it that he was shocked he hadn't identified her earlier. The flare and agility displayed was uniquely hers. And she should be uniquely his. But he didn't say that. He said the first thing that came to his mind when faced with the woman he wanted in his bed but couldn't have.

"What the hell?" he growled at her.

His first reaction was anger. Anger at her being here. In his manliest of places. Anger at her being here and him not knowing it. Anger that she was here, and yet he still couldn't think of how to get her back into his life.

And then anger that she was here to witness a defect, his cursed broken mask. He needed to fix it and return to the match.

"What?" she challenged. "You act like you've never seen me in my gear before."

"You know what the bloody hell I'm talking about. What the deuce are you doing here?"

"I came here to beat you. In front of everyone." She had a wicked gleam, laden with pain, in her eyes.

"This is... this is..." how should he finish that? *This is no place for a woman. This is a man's game. This is my world.*

Infuriated, he looked around, not seeing anything as it should be. He lifted his mask into the air. "I need a new one. Mine snapped."

"You poor man. Your mask broke. At least you still have a chance at winning." She scoffed. "You didn't trip over your own feet when it mattered the most not to."

Trip? On her own feet?

And then he saw it. She didn't know. And she blamed herself. Foolish, foolish chit. She was a fighter, but she couldn't see what she was fighting. Or maybe more accurately, who she was fighting. She couldn't see the truth about her match. Perhaps she couldn't see the truth about him either. She blamed herself. He saw it now. She blamed herself for his lies. She blamed herself for losing the match. But how could one blame her when all she had done was try? His anger seeped out of him.

"How can you be so blind yet so sharp at the same time?" he asked quietly.

"What are you talking about?"

"You didn't trip."

"The referee said I did—"

"He's being paid off. I'm not sure who's worse. The ref or Tamely. Tamely's a miscreant, a bounder, and a cheat. He tripped you. Didn't you hear the crowd booing?"

She looked stunned. "I thought they were disappointed in my performance."

"My God, Bodi. How could you think that? You're amazing. And…" *Perfect. Difficult. Irritating as hell, but irresistible.* "Wrong. They weren't booing at you, they were booing at him."

"If everyone knows it, then why don't they do something about it?"

"They might. But no one's going to call him out."

"Why not?"

Wesley scoffed. "Who knows? Not enough evidence? Pride? Fear? Maybe no one thinks he's worth it. If every enemy that man has made called him out, it would have been fatal long ago. He's just one of those weasels that gets away with bullying people. Some people can get away with murder." He shook his head. Pointing to her garb, he said, "Sorry you lost your round. Obviously it took great effort for you to be here."

"It's fine. It wasn't meant to be."

Wesley shuffled his mask between his hands, an idea forming

in his mind. An idea just outrageous enough to befit a warrior like Boudicca fighting for her *lost freedom and bruised body*.

"Maybe it was though." Maybe it was meant to be exactly as it was.

Maybe he was supposed to have bumped into her that fateful night. Maybe the gods had a plan. Maybe...he just needed not to be an arrogant arse.

"Take my place." He held out his sword.

"What?" She retreated a step, as if he were holding out stinking socks rather than a weapon, and a tool, to make her a champion.

"Go fence Samuel. And win. For me." He offered a smile. "No. Not for me. For you. You deserve this. You are the better fencer. The world should know. You came here wanting to beat me, but go beat the best of the best. If you won against me, you would have revenge. Revenge is sweet, but the taste doesn't last. Go win this for yourself."

Her silence was his answer.

"Bodi,"—he stepped closer to her and kneeled in front of her—"this is your passion. I have seen it and felt it. I have lived a part of it with you. I know, it's clouded now, but what happened between us was real." Gently, he wrapped a hand around her upper arm. "This is who you are. Let the world see the real you. Do not be ashamed. Be you. And they will love you." He had so much he wanted to tell her, like, *they will love you the way I do*, but he couldn't say more past the lump in his throat.

Still she said nothing, so he stood to his feet. Gazing down at her sitting frame, she seemed as solid as stone. His soft words would do nothing. He could read her so plainly. She was unconvinced, and he knew he had to provoke her.

Not provoke. No, he had to cut her. He had to push where he knew it would hurt. So he said three words that he could never take back.

"I dare you."

Her eyes narrowed to a thin blade as she ground out, "It's

yours to win."

"It's *yours* to win."

Her shoulders rolled back to straighten her spine. His words were either rolling down her back like water droplets on a leaf, or sinking into the dirt to find roots. He needed it to be the dirt. He needed to reach her roots, for her to open up to him again. He wanted to see her bloom where she should plant herself. Not just where the world told her to grow in secret.

He was offering her the tournament. The weight of the offer hung in the air between them. If she fought and won, the *ton* would have to recognize her skill. If he took the match, he could beat Samuel and reclaim his pride. But love couldn't be about pride. Could she see what he was offering her?

And just when he thought perhaps he had broken through her impenetrable wall, the wall he had once before cut a door in, walked through, and then locked himself out of, she spoke.

"No."

There was that word again. But this time it burned a hole into his heart. This time she wasn't saying no to him, she was saying no to herself. And he just could not abide that.

He shrugged, casting his last line. "I bet you'd lose anyway."

She shoved herself up from her chair and made toward the door. She was leaving. Of course she was. He was being a cad. What else could he say though? If he couldn't soften her into it, nor could he provoke her into it, what did he have left?

She reached the door and turned to glance back over her shoulder with daggers for eyes, "How. Much?"

"How much, what?"

"How much do you want to bet?"

CHAPTER TWENTY-ONE

BOUDICCA WAS PERSPIRING before she even stepped foot on the piste. Surely she would be recognized. Someone would notice she wasn't Wesley. But no one did. She felt a couple of glances, but maybe the fact that she was wielding his weapon confirmed her identity to them. Besides, more often than not people saw what they wanted to see, what they expected to see, not what was truly in front of them.

She had already been there a day and a half, but somehow it felt new. All eyes were on her. But it was as if she had a blank slate. They didn't see her for Boudicca. They saw her as Wesley. A man. A man who could do anything. A man who had options. A man who had power. But those resources should not be exclusive to men. She would show the world the options and power a woman could possess. Let the gossip ruin her. If it could, it would. And if it didn't, then that would be its own beast to contend with because then she would have to face herself and the future she had been putting off for so long.

With confidence, she stepped up to face Samuel. But it wasn't just Samuel. He was all the people who didn't believe in her. He was all the people who didn't think a woman could be strong. Agile. Athletic. He was all the men that had made her work twice as hard as a man to get half as much.

This was her battle. This was her war.

She would use her skill and then her brains to win it. For all the outraged daughters. For all the daughters who knew it was wrong for women to be subjugated. And for all the daughters who didn't know. For all the daughters who didn't know that they had the right to dream. To do. To become.

To become more than just a woman or a lady. To be seen simply as a person. Not for their beauty. Not for their skill. Not for their polite smile. Their curtsy or tea pouring abilities. A person to love and be loved.

It was altogether too much to put on a simple match. Yet still not enough.

The match had been reset and begun and Samuel aggressively advanced. He was direct. With a lightning fast lunge, he took the first point high outside. Rattled, Boudicca restarted. But her emotions were wound tight, and she was caught off guard. He quickly snagged a second point with nearly the exact same maneuver. He probably thought Wesley was a simpleton.

But to hell with that. She wasn't going down this way. By jove, she had come to fight. No, she had come to win. This was her chance. If she didn't pull it off, then it would all be for nothing. Wesley would have let her take his place only to secure him another loss. That was intolerable. She would not fail him. But even more importantly, she wouldn't fail herself.

She would not get this chance again. It was now or never.

She shuffled her sword and gracelessly moved forward in hopes that the awkward movement would distract Samuel. If it looked like she didn't know what she was doing, he wouldn't know how to prepare a defense or counterattack. One. The flop worked. His eyes didn't know where to focus, and she stole a point low inside. Quicker on the attack than even him, she snared a second point high outside. Two. When she struck, she heard his labored breathing, and she knew the win was within reach.

This was her time. She was not the kind to show off. To boast of her skill was considered improper for a lady. But right now she wasn't a lady. She was a fencer. And she was damn well going to be the best bloody fencer the *ton* had seen yet.

She readied herself for Samuel's aggressive lunge, and parried it away. She feinted right and moved left, letting him nearly go by her. He would turn quickly to strike, thinking he had won. In her mind's eye she could see him smiling. And then...

He didn't see it coming. He didn't have a chance. She swung her arm high and around, snagging him high outside on his shoulder.

Three.

The crowd erupted. Her signature move had the men, all of them, on their feet shouting praises. For as long as she could bear it, she let the shouting pour over her. The referee was on his way over to her to confer her medal. It was a moment for the ages. They had never seen anyone strike like that before. Let alone...a woman.

She tore off her mask and slammed it to the ground.

The referee became a statue. The crowd was in a second, even louder uproar. A woman. How can she fence? Where's the Duke of Baskim? Wait. Wait. Wait.

And then...

Hands were on her legs and around her waist. Wesley was there with James and Chris, and they were hoisting her upon their shoulders. It was scandal after scandal. But she didn't care. She had the support, literally, of three dukes beneath her.

The three, plus a mixed crowd, were cheering for her with the loudest voices and largest grins. Chris, the quiet one, she had least expected such boisterous support from. James, she knew the least, yet he had been the one to steady her on Wesley's and Chris' shoulders. And Wesley must have been watching the whole thing, for he had been at her side first. That thought thrilled her the most.

She glanced down to see that Samuel had an inscrutable glare reserved for her. Even amidst all the chaos, she saw Wesley nudge Samuel hard in the ribs. Then she overheard him hiss at his friend, "You can get your arrogant arse over here to support my future wife, or you can stand there like an imbecile who just lost to a woman."

Or perhaps it was that threat that thrilled her the most.

AFTER HER TRIUMPH, Wesley used his carriage to take Boudicca home. They sat in her drawing room with tea between them. It had been such a rush to see her beat Samuel, though he had no doubts that she could, that this moment felt far too serene.

"You must know that you won't receive the medal."

"Yes, I figured."

"And they'll probably redo the tournament."

"That makes sense."

"But everyone knows you beat him. Fair and square."

Her smile warmed his heart. "I suppose some people will try to spread gossip that it was all a scheme."

"There are conspiracies about everything. It's bound to happen."

"People will say anything, but the majority will know the truth." It was optimistic, but he still hoped it would play out that way. "Rest assured that anyone wanting to remain in good favor with the four of us dukes will agree upon the truth that a woman is the best fencer in London."

"Even if only a few know the truth, that's more than before. I've come a long way." She took a sip of tea.

"We both have." He sighed, wanting to tell her so much, and knowing this was the time to do it. "I need you to know something about me. My standards are so high because of my father. He had to have the best, and he made it known that I had to be the best. He drilled it into me that winning was everything. He would always tell me not to come home unless I won."

"He couldn't be serious, could he?"

"Locked-me-out-of-the-house-and-sent-me-away serious."

"I see."

"I'm telling you this because I feel as though today I finally saw Boudicca in all her fullness." He raked a hand through his hair. "And...I want you to see me more fully because well, I want us to fully see each other." It was not as smooth as he had intended, but it was just the way the words tumbled out.

Her raised brow invited him to add more to his already eloquent speech.

"I know you must hate me. I deceived you. There's no excuse for it. It was one of the most imbecilic actions I've ever taken. But truth be told, it was the *best* most imbecilic action I've ever taken as well. Fate intervened and led me to you." He stood and walked around the table, then kneeled at her side and took her hand in his. "It led me to you. If I must beg your forgiveness every day, I will do so."

"In full transparency, I should tell you something about my sisters before you go any further."

"Tell me."

"We each have plans to snare ourselves a duke."

He waved his hand in the air. "That is nothing new."

"By any means necessary."

"Well, I'm sure you'll use your discretion." He looked up at her solemn eyes. "Won't you?"

"I can't speak for the other three, but I don't regret my actions."

"Neither do I. Now, really, I have something of utmost importance to ask you. I can't imagine another day without you. The last week has been hollow. I have missed my time with you. You are the most incredible woman I have ever met. You will make an excellent wife, an inspiring mother, and a formidable duchess. I have never told a woman this before, but...I love you." His heart was pounding, waiting to see if she felt the same way and to see if she would take the leap.

Her hand cupped his jaw, and he had to still his breathing.

"I love you, Wesley."

He gazed deeply into clear blue eyes, envisioning himself

with her forevermore. "Will you marry me?"

Her brows knit together as she looked around the room and then caught his eye, "Wait, did you not bring me flowers?"

THE NEXT EVENING Boudicca sat at the dinner table with her family laughing about the previous weekend.

She was recounting all of the events to them. "And he didn't return until he had flowers—"

"Pink peonies," Wesley pointed out.

"And chocolates."

"And a gift."

"Oh yes, a gift." Boudicca smiled.

"A gift? Bodi, it was the gift of the century."

"The century, really? Isn't that a bit overreaching?" she challenged him.

"Well, what do you call it when someone gifts his betrothed her dream gift? A building that she can use for fencing to her heart's delight? And so that she doesn't always have to come running home to her father's house—no offense Humphrey—to do what she loves?"

The sisters around the table let out soft chuckles.

"When did you tell him about your dream to open a fencing school for girls?" Mimi asked.

Wesley dropped his fork. "She never told me that." He turned to stare at Boudicca. "You want to instruct young girls to rebel against societal structures and follow in your footsteps?"

Boudicca nodded firmly.

He stroked his jaw. "So what you're saying is, I really did buy you your dream gift, and you didn't even have to ask for it?"

She nodded again.

"So it is actually the perfect gift for you?"

She nodded a third time. This time with tears in her eyes.

He reached over and pulled her into an embrace. "You silly gel. Why didn't you tell me about that?"

"I was trying to ease you into my future."

"Your future?"

"Our future."

"I didn't think you knew how to ease into anything. I thought you just always came out guns blazing."

"That's Zenobia," she chuckled.

"What?" Wesley asked in bewilderment.

"The guns," Boudicca explained. "Never mind. Thank you for the gift. It is perfect, and it's really the only reason I agreed to be your wife and create a future together."

"Well, it's our future, and I can't wait for more of it."

"So if he hadn't bought you the gymnasium you would have refused his offer?" Joan smiled, knowingly.

Boudicca only shrugged. "Well I did tell him that he also owes me half of what he wins for his silly little bet."

"What does he win?" Mimi asked.

"I have no idea, but it better be good."

Chapter Twenty-Two

The wedding took place three days later. One day to recover and collect a special license. One day to recover from recovering, and then the last day to say their *I do's*.

The day before the wedding, the day of recovering from recovering, was the most notable.

Wesley showed up with flowers (pink peonies) in one hand, and waving the special license in the air in the second hand. Sans chocolate. But she couldn't expect them upon every visit, could she?

Boudicca saw the waving paper and led Wesley up to her room before anyone else could join them.

"There's one last thing I want to do before we get married," she said in a soft voice, reminding him of the night he bumped into her. Before he really knew her. She had been all sweetness as a stranger, and then she had turned to stone. And then to ice. Then to fire wielding a sharp blade. And now back to sweetness. The woman would never cease to surprise him.

And with the warning that there was something else she wanted to do before marriage, Wesley felt his heart hammer in his chest. In his mind, he envisioned all kinds of requests. Larger gifts. An adventure somewhere. Taking up another hobby. Did the woman have another secret that he needed to know about? Was there another dream she had yet to mention? What was she going to show him? He had hoped that everything was out in the open since they had divulged their deepest dreams and pains to each other, but really, he just couldn't be sure. It was a tiny portion of him that was squirming, wriggling, curious. What was going to happen next? And he loved it. He loved her. So whatever she wanted to do, he was going to make sure she achieved it.

Really, that seemed the least he could do. He knew she had forgiven him. The begging had helped. The gift of the gymnasium had helped more. Now he wanted to show her how much he could love her.

"What do you want to do?" He asked as she tugged him into her bedchamber.

She closed the door. Locked it. And tossed the special license to her desk. "You."

Well, now...that was a request he could easily accomplish. He would work toward her achievement with ample effort. In fact, she may have a few achievements, if he had his way. Her eyes were glistening with delight, and he studied her lips, still rounded from the last word to leave them. And before he could part his own lips to offer any words of affection or seduction, he realized they wouldn't be necessary.

Her lips were already on his. Drunk in elation. Her breasts were flattened to his chest, and her legs were clamoring to climb him. A surge of joy shot through him.

"Boudicca, you are my greatest win. I will always be at home with you. There is no greater triumph than finding the love of your life and cherishing her."

"I didn't realize you were so romantic, Wesley."

"I'm not. But you do something to my heart that makes it..."

"Gush?"

"Apparently."

He lifted her up and waltzed over to the bed. A bed. Finally a bed, though he didn't imagine himself doing much sleeping in it. One by one, he withdrew the pins from gloriously golden tresses until finally her hair cascaded over down her shoulders. Her rosy pink lips parted in a gasp, and he could almost read her thoughts.

Remembering what they had already experienced together only a few nights ago. She was perfection, and he needed to see all of her. Slowly, he pulled the ties of her frock as she pointed them out. Not that he needed the instruction, but if she wanted to lead in parts, he wanted to follow. If she was willing to ask for what she wanted, he would be willing to give it to her.

He wriggled her out of her frock, and when she pointed to his chest with a half-smile, he began to slide his arms out of his jacket. When her finger motioned downward, he untied his cravat and unbuttoned his waistcoat and shirt, taking off the rest of his top layers.

Standing before her, chest bare, her smile widened. He could imagine those lips in a number of places. One of which was growing intensely hard. So when she crooked her finger and beckoned him closer, there was no hesitation.

He kneeled over her and weaved his hand through her hair. "You're beautiful, Bodi."

A small blush crept up her neck and he followed its path, wondering where it would end. Just above her breasts, he soon discovered. But that didn't inhibit his explorations downward. His kisses meandered south toward her two rolling hills and their peaks. Each one he took his time with. When he looked up at her half-lidded eyes, her moan and her hand in his hair directed him southward.

And if a man could climb the mountains, he could delight in the valleys.

Slowly he trailed his tongue down her soft, creamy stomach. Soft to lick, but firm to touch. His warrior was strong. He felt her flex as his tongue continued its journey. And there he found the soft tight curls and dewy mons where he lapped up her sweet nectar. God, she tasted divine.

"Wesley," she whimpered.

He longed to hear more. He could never hear enough.

"Mmm…you taste so good." He licked down her lips, into the valley and up the other side. Her moaning called to him.

"Not yet, Bodi."

He squeezed her bottom and she arched up into his face. Her desire set him ablaze and he found her sweet core, licking and sucking, until she nearly bucked him off.

Her panting, eager breaths quickened and then she gasped.

Her hands were grappling at his biceps, trying to yank him up and closer to her. "I want to feel you, Wesley," she whispered.

He laid himself atop her and she moaned into his shoulder. "I want to feel you inside of me, Wesley."

Reaching down he placed his shaft at her entrance and slid inside. God, how she felt like home. She was the most perfect accident to have happened to him. He couldn't have asked for a better counterpart. If he had tried to pick the perfect woman, he wouldn't have known where to start.

He had been trying—in some capacity—to find the perfect woman. He thought he knew what he wanted. But there was no way he could have known what he needed. She was delight. Challenge. Sparks. Propriety. Integrity. Loyalty. She would never back down. Never quit. She epitomized what it meant to win. For she had won her fights, and she had won his heart.

It wasn't something he had intended to give away. He had told the other three that they could plan his married life, not his love life, yet here he was. With a love life the size of…

He looked down. To see where their bodies were joined. His cock felt ginormous inside of her. He had never felt so huge, like a throbbing, aching mess. All for her. All for love.

"Wesley," she moaned.

And he thrust inside of her.

"Uhh…"

Her sounds impelled him to move faster. Still on his knees, his hands under her bottom, he tilted her up and the angle pulled him deeper inside of her.

"Bodi, you are my home," he growled. He need never sleep in a bed again, so long as he knew he had her.

And he watched as she shattered in his arms at the same time he spilled into her. Pure euphoria. Pure triumph. Pure love. Home.

Epilogue

The wedding was a simple affair.
Well, simple was one word. Peculiar. Eccentric. Downright strange. Those were other words, perhaps more aptly applied to this specific ceremony. There would have been more words had the couple invited the expected crowd. But they did not.

Thanks to the special license permitting them to marry in whichever location they selected, the ceremony took place in the gymnasium. The Practice Hall. Flowers abounded. Boudicca had chosen the flowers gladiolus and nasturtium to signify victory, and hyacinth to signify sports and games. Red roses were placed to represent love, and of course there were also pink peonies which happen to mean happy life.

When the couple walked down the piste, Boudicca was on her father's arm. Humphrey had kept his handkerchief accessible, as he found himself wiping his eyes on several occasions. The first of which was when Boudicca whispered in his ear that she had reached for her destiny and found it to be more than she could ever have dreamed. He had kissed her cheek saying she looked stunning and wouldn't her mother be proud.

Boudicca was in all white with lace trim, wearing her mother's dress that had been altered slightly to fit her.

Points went to Boudicca for not wearing her gear for the ceremony, though she managed to hold her rapier along with her bouquet. In fact, it was the gift she presented to Wesley when she reached the end of the aisle-slash-piste. The offering had caused a few chuckles to emerge from the guests. But Wesley received it with pride and honor. And a large smile.

She meant it to convey her commitment to him. That what was hers was also his now. That they would fight together. Practice together. Win and lose together. They were a team. If one of them lost, they both lost. If one of them won, they both won.

And somewhere in the ceremony, the vicar allowed them to make such promises to each other. Boudicca had been misty eyed when she voiced them, and she was fairly sure she saw a sheen in Wesley's eyes as well.

The three sisters were exchanging dark-trimmed handkerchiefs to wipe tears from their eyes while Wesley's three grooms were discreetly (not so discreetly) exchanging billfolds and coins to line their pockets. It was not unexpected behavior.

The gathering was small though; only family and a few friends were invited. The size and space allowed for the intimacy Boudicca craved. This event didn't need to be a show. She had already had that. This event needed to be about the people closest to her. And it need only be a space filled with love, not whispering or gossip.

The pronouncement of husband and wife caused a sigh to release from her. She had a husband now. A man she could trust. Finally. Yes, he had had his ulterior motives. Perhaps it was too much to ask for perfection. To ask for an angel. A man with no stains. But those stains, his failures, his weaknesses made him human. And she had fallen for him. Motives and all. And he loved her, secrets and all.

It was too easy to forgive him once she knew that he loved her. He was a man of honor and integrity and was willing to make amends for his mistakes. That's all she could ask for in a man and a partner for life. Love. A love that was willing to fight. A love that would triumph.

After the ceremony, the guests were milling around waiting to be fed. It was the perfect moment to steal Wesley away. They wouldn't be missed. No one would notice. Well, everyone would notice. But no one would care.

"There's just one thing I want to do first as a married couple."

"What's that?"

"You'll see."

About the Author

Eliana Piers, award-winning and international best-selling author, has been writing and singing stories since she was five years old. After feeling inspired by authors like Julia Quinn, Tessa Dare, and Minerva Spencer, Eliana decided to test her quill on the page.

Writing about love and how two people come to connect and share parts of their souls with each other is now an obsession.

It's not worth it if you don't laugh, learn, or love while you're in it.

Eliana lives in Canada where she drinks an iced cap every day.

www.ingramcontent.com/pod-product-compliance
Ingram Content Group UK Ltd.
Pitfield, Milton Keynes, MK11 3LW, UK
UKHW020205270125
454178UK00010B/448